HEATHER'S CHOICE

In Memory of
Holly Fearon

HEATHER'S CHOICE

by

Carole Gift Page

Lake Shore Baptist Church

MOODY PRESS
CHICAGO

To my own
Kim, David, and Heather

© 1982 by
CAROLE GIFT PAGE

All rights reserved

Library of Congress Cataloging in Publication Data

Page, Carole Gift.
  Heather's choice.

  Summary: Although twelve-year-old Heather is somewhat
confused by her best friend's interest in boys, she is stunned
to learn her older sister has compromised her Christian
values for what she thought was love.
  [1. Sexual ethics—Fiction. 2. Christian life—Fiction]
I. Title.
PZ7.P137He   [Fic]   82-3417
ISBN 0-8024-3490-8   AACR2

2 3 4 5 6 7 Printing/LC/Year 87 86 85 84 83

Printed in the United States of America

1

Heather, Heather,
Light as a feather!
Has a face that
Looks like leather!

Heather Blake sat on the front porch steps polishing her good school shoes. She looked up and scowled when she heard Bobby's teasing, singsong voice.

"Heather, Heather, light as a feather," he chanted again, as he skimmed past her house on his skateboard a second time.

Heather jumped up and put her hands on her hips, pretending outrage. "Robert Cooper, you go take a long walk off a short pier!" Hearing a clinking sound, she glanced down. Oh, no! She had tipped over the bottle of brown polish. "Look what you made me do!" she shouted at the blond, laughing boy. He waved back gleefully.

Heather ran into the house for some paper towels. Her mother was in the kitchen by the stove, frying chicken, and the yummy, spicy aroma almost made Heather forget her anger—but not quite. "I hate boys," she announced, pulling several towels off the cardboard spindle.

5

"Boys?" questioned her mother, smiling. "Or Bobby Cooper in particular?"

"Well, if they're all like Bobby, you can have them. He's always pestering me!"

"Maybe that's just his way of showing you he likes you," suggested her mother.

Heather pretended to gag. "Please, Mom, don't say such a thing. He makes my skin crawl." Impulsively she reached for a hot, crisp drumstick on the platter, but her mother shook her head firmly.

"Put that back and wait for dinner," she said.

"Wait, wait, wait," complained Heather, only half in jest. "That's all I ever hear. I could collapse and die of starvation around here, and you'd say, 'Wait for dinner.'"

"No smart talk, young lady," said her mother. "Go tell Donna we'll be eating soon. She's probably upstairs rehearsing."

"Again?" asked Heather incredulously. "She must know that play backward and forward."

"This *is* opening night, remember."

I'd be scared out of my wits, mused Heather. "Imagine, getting up in front of all those people and trying to remember so many lines. I'd die!"

Her mother glanced at the paper towels in Heather's hand. "What are those for?"

"Oh, my goodness!" cried Heather, remembering the spilled polish. She dashed for the front porch, arriving just in time to see Bobby wiping up the last of the spill with his handkerchief.

"What are you doing here?" she blurted.

"Cleaning up after you." He looked at her, his gray-blue eyes twinkling. "How come you're so sloppy?"

Heather made a face. "How come you're so—so disgusting?"

He grinned. "Better watch out. It'll freeze like that."

"What?"

"Your face. You'll go around looking like this." He crossed his eyes and stretched his mouth outrageously with his fingers.

Heather laughed involuntarily. "Boy, what an improvement! Bobby Cooper, you never looked so good."

Bobby's expression grew momentarily serious. "Want to come over and play Scrabble?"

"No. You'd probably cheat. Besides, I can't anyway."

"Why not?"

"The junior class play is tonight, and my sister is the *star*. The whole family's going."

Bobby laughed with amused surprise. "Donna—a star? I just bet. I guess next you'll tell me she's going to Hollywood."

"No," said Heather, "but she could be a great actress if she wanted to. Everybody says she's good. She has *talent*."

"Talent? Oh, wow. *Talent*!"

"That's a word you probably never heard of," snapped Heather.

Bobby ignored the insult. "So what's the play?" he asked offhandedly.

"Thornton Wilder's *Our Town*. Donna plays Emily."

"Never heard of it."

"You never heard of anything that wasn't in a comic book!" said Heather smugly. "*Our Town* is

7

about a boy and girl who fall in love and get married."

"Ugh!" Bobby grimaced. "A mushy love story." He then assumed a mocking tone: "And they lived happily ever after."

"No," Heather said thoughtfully, "there's more to it than that. The story is sad and wonderful all at once. Emily dies, but she comes back to earth to relive her twelfth birthday. She sees that people here don't appreciate all the things they have. But then it's not the sort of play *you* would understand."

Before Bobby could shoot back a sarcastic reply, an insistent voice sounded from inside the house. "Heather! Dinner's ready! Get Donna!"

Heather opened the screen door, then glanced back at the lanky youngster. "See you later, Bobby—if I'm that unlucky."

The youth picked up his skateboard. "Sure, Heather Feather—unless I see you first."

Heather went inside and took the stairs two at a time. Entering the room she shared with her older sister, she stopped short and gazed admiringly at Donna, who stood posing in a white dress before the full-length mirror.

"You look gorgeous," exclaimed Heather, her eyes scanning her sister's dark curls and roses-and-cream complexion.

Donna didn't seem to hear her. Her eyes had a distant look. Then suddenly she relaxed and turned to Heather with a smile. "I didn't see you come in."

"You were a million miles away."

"I know," replied Donna, her voice soft and

light. "I was rehearsing. I was Emily—in Grover's Corners—the third act. I had just left the cemetery on the hilltop to go back home and relive my twelfth birthday. It was an ordinary day, but so beautiful and so painful. No one could see me. I kept saying, 'Mama, Papa, it's me, Emily. I'm here. Look at me.' But they just went about their business. They couldn't hear me because I was dead. And they didn't understand how wonderful life is, even the little things."

Heather sighed wistfully. "You've got me really believing you're Emily."

Impulsively Donna embraced her sister. "This is the most wonderful—and frightening—night of my life. It has to be right. I have all these wildly fantastic dreams inside of me—"

"You'll be great. Everyone says so."

Donna paused and scrutinized her reflection. Then she smiled. "But I couldn't do it if it weren't for Randy. He makes a perfect George."

"George?"

"You know. George Gibbs, Emily's husband in the play. We work together so well. Wait'll you see the part where we say our wedding vows. Oh, Heather, I adore Randy. He makes this play so special for me—he makes everything so special."

Heather smiled knowingly. "Sounds to me like somebody's in love."

"Don't tell anyone," cautioned Donna breathlessly. "It's our secret, OK?"

"Well, you look just like a bride in that dress," murmured Heather approvingly. "Why can't I look like you? Why do I have to be a skinny, awkward twig?"

"You'll grow. Give yourself time."

"Yeah. A hundred years! I'm the only girl in seventh grade still wearing undershirts."

"You're only twelve. Don't rush things."

Heather attempted a glamorous pose before the mirror. She looked like a silly kid. *If only I could just skip the next few years and be sixteen like Donna,* she mused.

"You girls get down here to dinner, this instant!" their mother called impatiently from the foot of the stairs.

Donna gasped. "I can't eat fried chicken in this dress. Hurry, Heather, unzip me!"

Minutes later the girls arrived at the table and slipped contritely into their seats. Their father gave them a mildly scolding glance, then reached for their hands. He bowed his head and said, "Lord, we thank You for this food and for making Meg such a great cook."

Heather didn't look up, but she imagined Dad was smiling. He liked sneaking in compliments while asking the blessing.

"And help Donna in the school play tonight," he continued. "We know she'll do a fine job for You, Father. We all love You and thank You for being our Savior. Amen."

"And don't let me forget my lines," added Donna under her breath. She looked around. "Come on, everybody, eat fast. I have to be at the auditorium by seven."

"Chew *slow-ly,*" corrected Mother, accenting every syllable. "We don't want indigestion."

The school play was scheduled for 8:00 P.M. The Blake family, arriving at seven, was able to

10

get good seats in the third row.

There's not even a fat lady with a puffy hairdo to block my view, Heather noted with relief.

Promptly at eight, the curtain opened. Heather stared in surprise at the stage. "There's no scenery," she whispered to her mother. "Just a table and a few chairs."

"That's how Mr. Wilder wrote it," her mother whispered back.

Even without elaborate props and scenery, the play was marvelous. Donna—Emily—looked like a lovely, delicate angel. Heather had never felt so proud of anyone in her life. She wanted to stand up and shout, "Hey, everybody, that's my sister!"

By the third act, Heather felt as if she herself were a citizen of Grover's Corners, grieving over Emily and the other townspeople who were buried in the little hilltop cemetery.

As the play drew to a close, Emily stepped to the center of the stage and said in a clear, full voice, "Good-by, world. Good-by, Grover's Corners—Mama and Papa. Good-by to clocks ticking . . . and Mama's sunflowers."

Heather sniffed loudly.

Emily talked on, bidding the world farewell. Then she gazed out at the audience and asked meaningfully, "Do any human beings ever realize life while they live it?—every, every minute?"

Heather, listening intently, resolved right then that she would realize life every moment—as soon as she figured out just what that meant. It was obvious that Donna knew. Tonight, as the curtain lowered and the audience applauded,

Donna had the whole world right in her hands.

Heather clapped loudly, until her palms stung. She felt fiercely proud of her sister and—maybe, if she admitted it—just a tiny bit envious.

2

To celebrate Donna's successful performance in *Our Town,* Meg and Jeffrey Blake took their two daughters to the lake on Saturday. It would be a special day, their first picnic of the year.

Heather brought along her best friend, Pam Morrow, a blonde, bubbly girl from her class. Pam was tall for her age and shapely for a seventh grader—a fact that distressed Heather when she thought of her own Popsicle-stick shape.

The two girls had known each other since third grade and had vowed to be best friends forever. They had even written down their commitment on notebook paper, sealed it in an envelope, and buried it in the woods halfway between their homes. I, HEATHER BLAKE, PROMISE TO HAVE NO BEST FRIEND BESIDES PAM MOR-ROW—FOREVER. Pam promised the same.

Donna came to the picnic with Randy Gordon, who had portrayed her husband George in the play. Randy was very tall, with a rich, tanned complexion, a deep voice, and dark, laughing eyes. He was always smiling, as if he had a special secret he was eager to share.

Heather was surprised to find that she enjoyed watching Donna and Randy together—the way they gazed tenderly at each other or linked hands as they strolled by the lake. Or the way they stood talking confidentially, their heads together, absorbed in a private world no one else dared to enter.

Not that Heather wished to intrude anyway. She was perfectly satisfied to watch from a safe distance, observing unnoticed. *Romance is a curious thing,* she thought, *appealing and yet scary. An unknown factor.* Heather preferred to think of love in terms of storybook people—for instance, Emily and George in *Our Town.* In fact, fairy tales were even better. They always began "Once upon a time . . ." and ended ". . . happily ever after." Heather knew what to expect from them. She liked to imagine Donna and Randy like that, like Snow White and Prince Charming, two beautiful people destined to live happily ever after.

"Heather, you're doing it again."

Heather looked over in surprise at her friend Pam. "What?"

"You're staring at them—the lovesick couple. If we aren't careful, they'll send us to the store for ice cream so they can be alone."

Heather felt her face reddening. "I didn't mean to stare. They just look so happy together. I don't think they even know we're alive."

"Maybe not," conceded Pam. "But my older brother always sends me out of the living room when his girl friend comes over. I collect a lot of dimes that way."

Heather wrinkled her forehead. "Oh, come on. You're kidding."

"No, I'm not." Pam jauntily lifted her chin and

14

smiled. "Maybe I should raise my price to a quarter."

"Hey, girls, we could use some help!" called Heather's father as he carried a plate of sizzling hamburgers from the grill. "Help your mom set the table."

Heather and Pam ambled over to the picnic table where bowls of potato chips, baked beans, and macaroni salad were already spread tantalizingly on the red and white checkered oilcloth.

"Hey, Mom, what can we do to help?" asked Heather.

"You're too late to help set the table," replied her mother with feigned gruffness. "But you can sit down and help eat."

"That's what I'm best at anyway." Heather laughed, sliding onto the roughhewn bench.

After lunch, Heather noticed Donna and Randy across the table, exchanging several mysterious glances. *What's up?* she wondered silently. Finally Donna cleared her throat, making a deliberate sound. "Randy, why don't you run to the car and get the watermelon we brought," she said sweetly. "I'd love a slice right now."

Randy nodded, stood up, and strode toward the parking area. When he was out of earshot, Donna said eagerly, "I have something wonderful to tell you all."

While everyone looked Donna's way, Heather reached for another potato chip and popped it into her mouth. But the crunching sound seemed especially loud in the sudden silence. Donna glanced at her and waited impatiently until Heather swallowed with an obvious gulp.

15

Donna spoke again, her face glowing. "Randy and I—we've decided to—to go steady," she said, extending her hand to reveal Randy's class ring. "Isn't it gorgeous? You all are the first to know."

Heather gulped again, this time from surprise. She looked quickly at her parents. They were surprised too. More than surprised.

"Steady?" repeated her father. "Isn't this a bit sudden?"

"No, Daddy," replied Donna intently. "Randy and I have worked together in the play for weeks and weeks. We feel like we really know each other well."

"Donna, dear, I wish you'd talked this over with us first," interjected her mother. She sounded worried.

"Oh, Mom," groaned Donna. "You're not going to say no, are you? We're old enough. I'm sixteen and Randy's seventeen. We know what we're doing."

"You *think* you know what you're doing—"

"Mom, Randy and I care about each other—and we're both Christians. Doesn't that make a difference?"

Heather's father looked thoughtfully toward the automobiles. Randy was already striding back with the melon. "I don't doubt your feelings for each other," he told Donna at last. "But steady dating can bring special problems and pressures of its own."

"Oh, Daddy," she scoffed, "we're practically adults. You have to let me grow up sometime."

Heather's parents exchanged questioning glances.

"What do you think, Meg?"

"I don't know, Jeff. I admit I really don't know a nicer boy Donna could date."

"Then it's settled," said Donna happily. She greeted Randy with a triumphant smile.

Everyone looked from Donna to Randy as he set the watermelon gingerly on the table. He glanced around uncomfortably, realizing all eyes were on him.

"Randy, I told them," said Donna, beaming. "I told them we're going steady—and they approve!"

Randy's face reddened. "Great," he mumbled, thumping the watermelon nervously. It began to roll toward the table's edge, but he caught it with an awkward lunge. He finally managed to steady it, then sat down in embarrassed silence beside Donna.

"Hey, let's celebrate!" exclaimed Heather. She raised her paper cup of Kool-Aid in mock salute.

"Here's to the happy couple," crooned Pam, lightly tapping Heather's cup with hers. Some of the red liquid sloshed over the cardboard rim into the macaroni salad.

Donna made a face and said teasingly, "Why don't you girls go jump in the lake?"

"Sounds like a good idea to me," said Heather, scooting off the bench.

"Not before you help me clear the table," interrupted her mother.

"Aw, we almost escaped," Heather quipped, nudging Pam.

Later, Heather and Pam walked down by the lake, looking for a shallow, sandy place to wade.

17

Unexpectedly they spotted Donna and Randy, off by themselves, exchanging a lingering kiss.

"Oh, oh, I have a feeling we're not welcome company right now," remarked Pam wryly. The girls pivoted and walked back the way they had come. Strangely, Heather's face felt warm. She felt—what was it, embarrassed?—for Donna. "I thought you were supposed to wait until dark to kiss like that," she mumbled, staring at the ground as she walked.

"Who told you that?" quizzed Pam.

"No one. I just figured—"

"What do you know about kissing?"

"Nothing. I never have—not a boy, I mean—not like that."

"Would you like to?" asked Pam slyly. "I mean, if there was a boy you really liked?"

Heather looked quickly at her friend. "No. No, not ever. Would you?"

"Oh, well, no, I guess not. Not now, anyway."

"It'll be a million years before I kiss a boy like that," said Heather flatly. "A million years."

Pam shrugged uncertainly. "That's—well, that's a long time. I don't think I'd mind—I mean, if there was somebody neat—somebody really great. Not like the dumb boys in our class."

"They're all dumb—every boy I know." Heather scowled. "Except Randy. He's special. Donna's lucky to have him."

"Yeah," agreed Pam. "I'd like to find someone like Randy—someday."

Heather studied Pam's expression. Solemnly she said, "I don't think we should date boys until we're at least sixteen."

"Why sixteen?" asked Pam, sounding vaguely disappointed.

"Because I don't want any friend but you, Pam. I don't want us going around yammering about dating and kissing and stuff like that, like the boy-crazy girls at school. They make me sick, the way they blabber on, like no one in the world was ever in love but them."

The girls walked along in silence for a moment. Then Pam said reflectively, "I wonder what it's like to be in love."

"It's like magic," replied Heather without hesitation. "That's what Donna says."

"If you think it's so great, why should we wait until we're sixteen to date?"

Heather's brow furrowed. "I don't know. Maybe because being in love isn't just magic. It's scary, too. It's part of being grown up."

Pam nodded. "That's what I want—to be grown up. I hate people treating me like a kid."

"Sometimes I want to be grown up more than anything," said Heather thoughtfully. "But other times I never want to grow up."

"Yeah, it's a real pickle, isn't it?"

Heather looked blankly at Pam. "A pickle?"

"Yeah, you know. Life. It's one big pickle."

Heather laughed. "I can just see it. This gigantic green pickle, as big as the whole world."

"With a sign on top that says, 'Life is a pickle,' " added Pam.

"Maybe we could even market them," quipped Heather. "You know, like the pet rocks the stores sold a few years ago."

"You mean, a *pet pickle?* It'll never go!"

"Sure it will," argued Heather. "Be the first in your neighborhood to own your very own pet pickle. You don't have to feed it, wash it, brush it, or train it. It even comes house-broken!"

"You've been watching too many television commercials," hooted Pam. "Besides, all this talk about pickles is making me hungry."

"Hungry? We just ate!"

"That was a half hour ago," said Pam. "How about if we walk over to the pavilion and get a milkshake?"

"OK," replied Heather. "Let me tell Mom first."

Minutes later, the two girls followed the contour of the lake for a half mile until they reached the sprawling pavilion, made of timeworn, weather-beaten timber. The bright concession stands inside provided a welcome contrast to the structure's dark exterior. There were pool tables, a soda fountain, a place to purchase swimming gear, a row of pinball machines, and a roped-off area for shuffleboard.

Heather and Pam slipped onto the high counter stools and ordered chocolate shakes. While sipping their drinks, they turned and watched the people milling around them. Several children in wet swim suits were buying ice cream and cotton candy. Two bikini-clad girls stood watching while several lean, bronze-skinned men played shuffleboard. A teenage boy put a coin in the jukebox and the walls suddenly vibrated with a loud beat. Only the brassy clatter of the pinball machines competed with the surging music.

"This place is really something," said Pam approvingly. Her eyes strayed to two teenage boys

20

who had just entered the pavilion. Heather followed Pam's gaze, then looked away quickly when one of the boys caught her glance.

"We'd better be heading back," Heather told Pam as she slid off the stool.

"What's the hurry?" asked Pam.

The two boys approached the counter. They were wearing cut-off jeans and T-shirts imprinted with a brand name of beer. The taller boy pushed a mop of honey-brown hair from his eyes and drawled, "You girls aren't leaving, are you?"

"Yes," said Heather abruptly.

Pam made no effort to move. "Who wants to know?" she asked in a light, singsong voice.

"Me and Doug," replied the youth. "My name's Freddie. Freddie Vance."

"I'm Pam. This here's Heather."

The boys nodded and grinned pleasantly. Heather, her lips tightly pursed, merely blinked her greetings.

"You girls live around here?" asked Doug, his voice unexpectedly shifting from low to high in mid-sentence.

Pam pretended not to notice. "We don't live too far," she said offhandedly.

"What's your school?" asked Freddie.

"Westlake Junior High."

"Hey, Doug, don't we know someone from Westlake?"

"Yeah. Ginny something. You two know a girl named Ginny?"

"No," said Heather, nudging Pam impatiently.

"Wait. Maybe we do. What's her last name?" asked Pam.

"Jones—or Jenkins. Something like that."

Pam looked at Heather. "Don't we know a Ginny Jenkins? In math class?"

"I don't know," said Heather, flustered, shaking her head. The two boys kept watching her, smiling. "We better go, Pam," she said again. She winced at the whining sound in her voice.

Pam tossed her an irritated glance. "In a minute, Heather."

"Yeah, what's your hurry, Heather?" said Doug, his tone mocking.

"We've got some time to kill," added Freddie, sitting down next to Pam. "You girls want to play some pool?"

"Maybe."

"Pam, *please!*" Heather nearly shouted.

The two boys stared at Heather in momentary surprise. "Hey, you sure got a loud mouth for such a skinny little girl," remarked Freddie. The boys broke into raucous laughter. Pam joined in, too, with a forced, unamused chuckle.

Fighting back tears of humiliation, Heather turned and ran out of the pavilion. Moments later Pam caught up with her and demanded breathlessly, "What's the big idea?"

Heather sniffed loudly. "Suppose you tell me."

"What are you talking about?"

"The way you acted."

"Me? How about the way *you* acted!"

"Pam, those boys were complete strangers—"

"They were just being friendly. What's wrong with that?" snapped Pam. "You acted like they were untouchables."

"You were flirting with them."

22

"I was not! We were just talking. At least I didn't act like a dumb bunny."

Heather looked stricken. "How can you say that? You know we have to get back."

"That's just your excuse," muttered Pam. She looked appraisingly at Heather. "You can't be a kid forever, you know. Someday you'll have to talk to boys. If you always run away, how will you ever learn what to say?"

"That's not fair," countered Heather hotly. "I just didn't think we should be talking to boys we don't know."

"All I know," grumped Pam, "is I was having fun. Why weren't you?"

Heather didn't reply. She had no answer. All she was sure of was that for her the whole incident at the pavilion had been painful and embarrassing. She wanted to forget it and capture again the good-natured frivolity she and Pam had enjoyed earlier that afternoon. But for the moment, she couldn't think of anything funny to say.

3

"Heather Feather, you in there? Come on out!"

Heather took her time walking across the living room to the screen door. She could see Bobby Cooper, his face pressed against the fine screen netting, peering inside. He looked funny, his features flattened grotesquely. But his nosiness irritated her. *Why can't he simply knock politely, like other people?*

"What do you want, Bobby?" she asked curtly. She was eating a carrot and she chomped loudly now, for his sake.

He refused to be perturbed. "How about going skating?" he said.

Reluctantly she unlocked the screen door and permitted Bobby to enter. "Can't go skating," she mumbled between bites.

"Why not?"

"Busy."

"Doing what?"

"Nothing—just busy eating this carrot."

"Then go get your skates," said Bobby, sounding exasperated.

She eyed him quizzically. "You paying?"

"Just my own way," he said quickly.

"Then I can't go. I'm broke."

24

Bobby frowned, his shoulders slumping in supposed defeat. "OK, I'll lend you the green stuff till next week."

"It's a deal," said Heather, her interest perking. She wasn't about to admit it, but a rather boring week had passed since the fun of last Saturday's picnic. Even going skating with Bobby Cooper sounded like an improvement.

"I'll have to call my mother at the church," Heather added, going to the phone. "Mom's helping to get stuff ready for Vacation Bible School next week."

Bobby nodded. "I know. My mom's there too. In fact, she volunteered *me* to help supervise the little kids at recess. Yuk!"

"I'll be helping too," said Heather. "With refreshments—passing out Kool-Aid and cookies." She paused thoughtfully. "This is the first year I'll be too old to attend the classes. It seems strange. I've gone to Bible School every summer since Kindergarten."

"Yeah, I felt that way last summer. But that's how it goes. Too old for some things, too young for others," quipped Bobby. "Now make your call and let's get going."

Bobby and Heather rode their bikes the five blocks to the Holiday Roller Rink. As they pedalled, Bobby remarked with an edge of sarcasm, "I've noticed Randy Gordon hanging around your house a lot lately. What'd your folks do—adopt him?"

"No, silly. He and Donna are going steady," replied Heather smugly, increasing her speed.

Bobby pedalled faster too. "So she finally

hooked him, huh? The poor dope. Doesn't he know nobody goes steady anymore?"

"What would you know about it, smarty?" countered Heather.

"Enough to know I'd never get trapped like that," snorted Bobby.

The two were still bickering as they arrived at the rink and wheeled their bikes over to the rack. Nor had their tempers improved minutes later as they sat in the spectator area lacing their skates.

"If you ask me, I think going steady is dumb," said Bobby.

"That's because you've never been in love," snapped Heather.

"And I suppose you have!"

"No," she admitted grudgingly, standing up and following Bobby onto the waxed hardwood floor. They merged smoothly with the other skaters, gliding together in step, side by side.

Heather wasn't about to let Bobby have the last word. "Donna and Randy make a perfect couple," she said with pride, "just like Emily and George in Donna's school play."

"That play sure filled your head with a lot of romantic junk," grumbled Bobby. "You used to be an OK kid, Heather, just like one of the guys. But lately you talk like a—a *girl*."

Heather's eyes narrowed angrily. "I *am* a girl, stupid!" Impulsively she skated ahead of Bobby, moving too quickly and narrowly missing several other skaters. For an instant she lost her balance and nearly toppled, but then she steadied herself and coasted smoothly. She glanced back and was pleased to see Bobby lagging far behind.

Heather relaxed. She let the beat from the loudspeakers fill her eardrums and pulsate in her head. The music was nearly overwhelming, but, for a change, she liked it. It drowned out the buzz of conversation, the constant whir of skate wheels, and even her own thoughts. She felt pleasantly dazed. She was wafting, drifting, almost hypnotized by the surging rhythm of music and motion.

The spell was broken when someone shouted, "Heather!"

She looked around, startled, and spotted Pam skating toward her.

"I didn't know you'd be here," said Pam brightly.

Heather shrugged. "Bobby talked me into coming."

"Bobby? You mean good neighbor Bobby down the street?" said Pam thickly.

"The one and only."

"Well, ditch him and come with us," suggested Pam.

"Come with who?" asked Heather, glancing around curiously.

Pam nodded toward several youths lined up at the concession stand. "See those guys? They're all ninth and tenth graders. And guess what! They invited little old me to a party this evening."

"Really? Where?"

"I don't know yet—but who cares? They're high schoolers, Heather. And they treat me just like one of them."

"But do you know them?"

"No, but today we just started talking like old

27

friends." Pam gently elbowed Heather and smiled knowingly. "They said I could bring a friend."

"Who?"

"You, silly. How about it?"

"Oh, no, I couldn't," said Heather.

"Why not?" argued Pam. "They'll have some terrific music—and who knows what else?"

Heather frowned. "That stuff just isn't my thing," she mumbled. She wanted to say more, but she couldn't find the words. It wasn't that she really disliked that kind of music, but the party probably wouldn't be the proper place for a Christian. That's what Mom would say, and Heather suspected she would be right. Of course, Pam claimed to be a Christian too and attended church sometimes, but that didn't seem to stop her from doing whatever she pleased.

"You won't change your mind then?" said Pam, her tone clipped.

Heather gazed reluctantly at her friend. They were barely moving now on their skates. "No, Pam, I'd better not," she said lamely. "I've been gone all afternoon, so Mom will want me home tonight."

"OK," replied Pam abruptly. "It's your loss." Before Heather could respond, Pam skated off in a huff toward the concession stand. With a flourish she took the arm of one of the boys waiting for her and they melded gracefully into the colorful stream of skaters.

A minute later, the music was interrupted by a man's voice announcing, "Advanced backward skaters only on the floor, please."

Heather noticed Bobby in the rush of skaters

heading for the sidelines and the concession area. He waved pleasantly at her, as if they had never exchanged harsh words earlier. "Want a Coke?" he called.

"Sure." They met in front of the popcorn machine, and Bobby ordered Cokes and a box of buttered corn. They made their way over to a bright orange table and sat down.

"For a while I thought maybe you had skipped out," Bobby remarked between mouthfuls of the fluffy kernels.

"No, I was right here."

"I saw you talking with your friend."

"You mean Pam?"

"Yeah. Isn't she supposed to be your best friend?"

Heather's brow furrowed. "Yes, I—I used to think so."

"What do you mean by that?"

"Nothing," replied Heather. She sipped her drink. She realized she was flattening her straw between her fingers.

"You have a fight with *her*, too?"

"No," said Heather quickly. "Why do you ask that?"

"No reason. But that girl—something about her gives me a pain. Maybe it's her attitude. She really thinks she's something. I just saw her over there with a bunch of high school guys—real wild ones, if you ask me."

Heather winced. "You mean that's what you think of them, too?"

Bobby glanced around cautiously, then returned his gaze to Heather. "I'm not trying to

29

worry you, really. It's just a known fact that those guys like to have a good time. That's all."

Heather shook her head slowly. "I just don't understand Pam," she murmured sadly. "We've been best friends since third grade. Now suddenly she's changing. She does such weird things. I can't figure her out. I don't understand the way she acts." Heather leaned across the table urgently. "What do you think is wrong with her, Bobby? Why has she become so—so boy crazy?"

Bobby shrugged and reached for more popcorn. As he swallowed a generous helping, he managed to declare, "As far as I'm concerned, Heather Feather, all girls are crazy anyway!"

4

Heather sat crosslegged on her bed, watching Donna lightly brush her cheeks with blusher and carefully apply mascara to her lashes. After several long moments of studying her reflection in the mirror, Donna turned to Heather and asked, "Is my lipstick too dark? I have a lighter shade."

"No, it looks great," said Heather. She smiled mischievously. "Besides, what difference does it make? It'll disappear when Randy kisses you."

Donna picked up her pillow and tossed it playfully at Heather. "Take a hike, skinny britches."

Heather caught the pillow and hugged it against her chest. "Where are you going tonight?"

A dreamy look softened Donna's eyes. "Randy is taking me to the Hawaiian Winds Restaurant," she said. "They have real Polynesian food—and everyone says it's terribly romantic."

"And expensive, I'll bet," whistled Heather. "How can Randy afford it?"

"He can't," answered Donna confidentially. "The rest of our dates this month will be at McDonald's. But it's worth it."

Heather smiled as her sister turned gracefully before the mirror. Donna reminded her of a lovely, dancing ballerina on a music box. "You sure do sound happy," remarked Heather.

"I *am* happy," said Donna, her voice lilting. She stopped and gazed earnestly at Heather. "I hope someday you're as happy as I am. Everyone in the world should be this happy."

The moment seemed magical. Heather felt warm to her toes with love and admiration for her sister. But the special moment was shattered suddenly by the doorbell.

"Oh, no! Randy's early," cried Donna, scooping her cosmetics into her evening bag.

"I'll go talk to him,"offered Heather, scrambling off the bed.

"No, wait," said Donna. "I'll go. Randy hates to have the family gawking at him. I promised I'd always be ready on time so he wouldn't have to stand around carrying on small talk with Daddy."

"I don't *gawk*," Heather defended.

"Well, you know what I mean," said Donna quickly as she went out the door.

"Yeah, well, don't bother to say good-bye," Heather grumbled as the door slammed shut. She went back over to the bed and sat down, feeling a little let down with Donna gone. And restless. Yes. She felt strangely restless. But why?

Heather stood up and walked over to Donna's bookcase. She removed the copy of Thornton Wilder's play *Our Town*. With a pleased smile, she decided that right after dinner tonight she would curl up in bed and read herself to sleep. It would be fun to become reacquainted with George and Emily and the people of Grover's Corners. Besides, she wanted to recapture the warm, wonderful feelings she had experienced while watching Donna on the stage, playing Emily. That had been an event Heather would never forget.

That evening Heather read for nearly two hours before reluctantly dozing off. She was awakened a short time later by an unexpected noise. Groggily she stirred and reached for her book. It had fallen on the floor. So that was the noise that had startled her. But no, there was something else, another sound. Someone else was in the room with her.

Heather sat upright. Finally, through the shadows, she spotted a pajama-clad Donna by the closet hanging up her clothes. She breathed a sigh of relief. But the relief turned back to anxiety as she heard Donna sniffling.

"Donna, are you all right?" Heather whispered.

Donna whirled around in surprise. "What are you doing awake?"

"I don't know," replied Heather. "I heard something. Are you—you're not—crying, are you?"

"No, of course not. What a dumb question. Go back to sleep."

Heather was wide awake now. "Did you have a good time tonight?"

"Yeah, just great," said Donna tersely.

"You sure? You sound funny."

Donna turned sharply. "Leave me alone, will you?" Her voice softened as she added, "I'm exhausted, Heather. I just want to get some sleep, OK?"

"But, Donna, I just wanted to let you know, I'm reading *Our Town*," said Heather, scarcely containing her enthusiasm. "It brings back all my memories of the school play, and of how super you were playing Emily."

"That's nice," Donna replied tonelessly. Without another word she climbed into her bed and turned her face to the wall.

"Didn't you have fun tonight?" persisted Heather with concern.

Donna didn't answer right away. "If you must know, we—Randy and I—had a—a disagreement," she murmured at last.

"A disagreement?"

"Yes, a—a difference of opinion, a quarrel."

Heather was silent, puzzled. She sensed that something more was wrong. But what? "I'll listen if you want to talk about it," she offered hesitantly.

Donna rolled over and raised up on one elbow. The moonlight etched one side of her face with a silvery glow. "Don't play Dear Abby with me, Heather," she warned. She paused, then added miserably, "But I'll give you some free advice. Don't ever think you can understand boys, because you can't. They make demands—push too far—then get mad for no reason. They're— they're impossible!" With that, Donna lay back down and pulled the covers up snugly around her.

Heather lay back too, cupped her hands under her head, and stared wide-eyed at the shadowy ceiling. A terrible sense of disappointment crept over her. What had happened to that lovely glow of romance surrounding her sister? Why had Donna and Randy fought? Apparently their beautiful relationship had a flaw. What a dismaying thought.

34

But a more distressing realization struck Heather. She and Donna had always been so close. Even with four years between them, they had freely shared their thoughts and feelings. But now, for some strange reason, Donna was shutting Heather out of her life. Was it possible that their treasured closeness as sisters was being threatened by an outsider—by a dumb boy?

5

For several days Heather struggled against a nagging sense of depression. She didn't know why she felt so blue. Was it because of Donna, or Pam, or just something puzzling inside herself?

Sometimes she stood in front of the hall mirror and pulled her shirt tight across her chest. Nothing. Absolute flatness. She looked like a yardstick. *At least Donna and Pam have curves. But I'll probably be eighty-two before I get any.*

On Wednesday, Heather's mother looked at her closely and said, "Why so glum?"

Heather shrugged. "Maybe I'm bored," she mumbled. That wasn't it, but she had no words to describe the real feeling.

"I have an idea," said her mother, smiling. "Why don't you invite Pam to stay over on Friday night?"

Heather brightened. "Really?" Then she remembered. "But what about Donna? She always complains that we keep her awake."

"She won't be here this weekend. Her friend Rachel invited her to go with her family to their cabin at the lake."

Heather whistled her surprise. "You mean Donna's going to be away from Randy for a whole weekend?"

"That's right." Her mother turned away to clear the lunch dishes. "Tell me, Heather," she began, choosing her words carefully, "has Donna said much to you lately?"

Heather thought immediately of last Friday night. But how could she explain Donna's moodiness when she herself was baffled by it?

When Heather made no reply, her mother continued. "I have a feeling that Donna was glad to have an excuse not to see Randy this weekend."

"Maybe she's not as in love with him as she thought," offered Heather, running water into the sink to wash the dishes.

Meg smiled grimly. "I hate to say it, honey, but I hope you're right."

Heather scarcely heard her mother's words. Her mind had wandered and was already brimming over with pleasant thoughts of Friday night's "slumber party" with Pam.

On Friday, Pam arrived at seven sharp in a sleeveless blouse and faded cutoffs, with an overnight bag under one arm and a bundle of records and games under the other. "I'm really not moving in for good, Mrs. Blake," she told Meg as Heather motioned her toward her room.

"Oh? Only for the summer then," joked Heather's father, looking up with a grin from his newspaper.

"This is a perfect night to stay over," said Pam, dropping her things on Donna's bed. "The weather's too warm to sleep anyway."

"I know. We can stay up all night," whispered Heather gleefully, "as long as we're quiet."

Pam sat down on the mattress with a bounce.

"We haven't gotten together like this for ages," she marveled.

"We'll have a super time," said Heather, bouncing down beside Pam. "What shall we do first?"

"I brought over some great records—some of the same songs they played at that party I went to."

Heather frowned as she recalled the party Pam had urged her to attend. That incident had caused a disturbing rift between them.

"It was a swell party," Pam went on excitedly. "And the way the kids danced, the way they moved and looked. I never danced like that before, so close with a boy. And they had colored lights flashing and one of those weird strobe lights. I felt like I was on another planet."

"Really?" said Heather, wrinkling her nose.

"Yes. You should have been there, Heather. The room was all dark except for these wild streaks of color on the walls and little revolving circles of light on the floor."

"It sounds like a nightmare I had once," said Heather dryly.

Pam's face settled into a pout. "Well, you're probably too young to appreciate it," she muttered.

"I'm only nine months younger than you," snapped Heather.

"Being grown-up has nothing to do with years," said Pam smugly.

Heather felt a sinking sensation. Somehow her perfect evening had veered off course. It was up to her to get back on track. She looked at Pam and pushed a smile into place. "Mom says we can make popcorn and milkshakes if we clean up the mess."

Pam's frown somersaulted into a grin. "Really? Then what are we waiting for?"

The two girls raced each other to the kitchen and began to gather the necessary items: butter, corn, cooking oil, a heavy iron skillet; milk, chocolate ice cream, the electric blender. Fifteen minutes later, they sat down on the front porch steps, the only cool spot around.

"This is the life," sighed Heather, munching corn and sipping her thick homemade shake. A slight breeze made goose bumps on her bare legs and arms.

When the girls had finished eating, they returned to Heather's room. Pam put one of her records on the stereo.

"Wait'll you hear this one," she said eagerly.

Heather shut the door so the music wouldn't disturb her parents. She knew they really didn't like the rock and disco sounds.

"I learned some dance steps too," said Pam, gyrating rhythmically to the pulsating beat.

Heather watched for a few minutes, then halfheartedly tried to imitate Pam's movements. After a while there was a knock on the door. Her father said, "Honey, it's getting a little late to play music that loud."

Pam looked perturbed as she lowered the volume on the stereo. "Now what can we do?" she grumbled.

"What games did you bring over?" asked Heather.

"Wait a minute. I have an idea." Pam walked

over to the phone on Donna's desk and picked up the receiver. "Where's your phone book? I have a plan that's an absolute riot."

Heather was skeptical. "You're not going to play that old trick of calling some grocery store and asking if they have pop in the bottle."

Pam laughed. "Oh, I know that one. When they say yes, you say, 'Then you'd better let him out.' "

"Or," said Heather, "is your refrigerator running? Then go chase it."

"I'm not playing those dumb games," declared Pam. Her eyes flashed cunningly. "Who's the cutest boy in our class?"

Heather thought a moment. "Mark Johnson is neat—or Paul Barker."

"Watch this," said Pam. She glanced through the phone book, found a number, and dialed. She cleared her throat and, lowering her voice an octave, she said, "Hello, Mark? You don't know me, but I'm a—a friend of a friend. I was wondering—what do you think of Heather Blake?"

Heather clasped her hands over her face, mortified.

"Oh, you think Heather's a nice girl?" continued Pam in her husky voice.

Heather dared to glance at Pam with one eye and giggled nervously.

"Well, what do you think of Pam Morrow?" Pam ventured.

Heather could no longer stifle her laughter. Pam began to giggle uncontrollably too. "Goodbye, Mark," she said hastily, and hung up the receiver. She glared at Heather. "Dummy! You made me laugh. Now I'll never know if he likes me."

"But what if he recognized your voice?" cried Heather.

"He didn't." Pam tried another number and asked for Paul Barker. A minute later she hung up. "His mother said he was at a Boy Scout camp for the weekend."

"So now what?" asked Heather.

"So now it's your turn," said Pam, handing Heather the receiver.

Heather shook her head. "No, thanks! Let's do something else."

"What?"

Heather gazed at Donna's dresser and smiled slyly. "We could try on some of Donna's make-up—if we're careful with it."

Pam didn't have to be invited twice. Eagerly she examined the bottles, tubes, and jars spread out neatly on Donna's bureau. The girls experimented with green and purple eyeshadow, bright pink and red lipsticks, mascara, and eyeliner. Finally they stepped back from the mirror and inspected the results.

"You look like that old-time movie star," Heather told Pam.

"Who? Joan Crawford?"

"No. Rin Tin Tin."

"Well, you look like Dracula," teased Pam.

Heather tried an imitation of the monster. "I vill bite your neck!" she droned ominously, curling her fingers like claws.

Her performance ended abruptly with an unexpected knock on the door. "Good night, girls," called her mother. "You two had better turn in pretty soon, too."

41

"Good night, Mom, Dad," said Heather. She looked at the clock on Donna's desk. Eleven already.

"I'm hungry again," said Pam. "Let's raid the refrigerator."

The girls stole quietly to the kitchen and made themselves cheese and bologna sandwiches.

"Let's watch the late show on television," suggested Pam, pouring herself a glass of milk.

Pam carried their snack to the living room while Heather checked the TV listings. "Listen to our choices," she said without enthusiasm. "There's 'Attack of the Giant Leeches,' 'Terror in the Haunted House,' or 'Curse of the Vampire.' "

"Maybe we should just eat and go to bed," said Pam reluctantly.

Heather nodded. Her eyelids felt heavier than she cared to admit.

But later, once she was in bed, Heather squinted through the darkness toward the other bed. "Pam? You awake?"

"Yeah. You too?"

"Yeah. It's too hot to sleep."

"What are you thinking about?" asked Pam.

"Nothing much," said Heather. "I was just thinking of snow and how good it would feel right now. How about you?"

Pam was momentarily silent. Then she said, "I was thinking about Dave Powers."

"Who's he?"

"The boy who took me to the party—a ninth grader." Pam's voice took on a reverential tone. "He—he kissed me, Heather."

Heather felt a catch in her throat. "Kissed you? When?"

"At the party. I didn't expect it. It was just—suddenly there he was, kissing me."

Heather couldn't keep the disappointment out of her voice. "I thought we were going to wait—"

"That was your idea," said Pam.

"What was it like?" asked Heather quietly.

"Nice. I'd do it again."

Heather turned her face to the wall, hot tears brimming in her eyes. She would never let a boy kiss her. The idea was repulsive. She wanted to ask Pam how she could do it—kiss a boy—and then speak of it with such apparent pride. But she remained silent. Just asking Pam the question would underscore the difference between them now. Somehow Heather felt left out—left behind. She reflected sadly, *Both Pam and Donna are growing away from me—all because of boys. Dumb boys! Why can't life be as simple as it used to be?*

6

When Donna returned home from her weekend at the lake, her first questions were about Randy. "Did he call? Have you seen him?" she asked Heather anxiously.

"No," Heather replied to both questions.

Donna spent most of Monday evening in her room talking on the phone with Randy. She kept the door shut, obviously wanting privacy.

"Well, looks like things are back to normal," Heather told her mother as they washed dishes together.

Meg looked concerned. "I had hoped—" she began, but her words trailed off. Heather had a pretty good idea what she was about to say.

"I don't care if that girl does have her own phone," said Dad, pouring himself a glass of iced tea. "She shouldn't stay on it all evening."

"I'll speak to her," said Mother, drying her hands on a towel.

During the next two weeks, Donna and Randy dated frequently. It seemed that every time Heather saw them, they were kissing or wrapped in each other's arms. They acted as if the rest of the world didn't exist. Heather didn't like that. She didn't like the way Donna drifted dreamily around the house, lost in thought. Sometimes Donna acted as if Heather were invisible. At other times she became unusually impatient and irritable with Heather.

"Keep out of my makeup, understand, Heather?" she'd snap. "Leave my things alone. Stay on your side of the room."

Heather started avoiding Donna. She never knew for sure what her sister's mood would be. Would Donna look right through her, unaware of her presence? Or would she explode in anger for no reason?

One evening Heather overheard her parents talking with Donna in Dad's study. She knew she shouldn't listen, but she remained by the door anyway.

"Donna, is anything wrong?" her mother questioned.

"No," said Donna crossly. "Why do you ask?"

Dad cleared his throat and said, "You must admit, sweetheart, you haven't been yourself lately."

"Yes, I have," Donna answered defensively.

"No, honey," replied Dad. "You've either been on edge or absorbed in your own little world."

"Are you feeling OK?" asked Mom.

"Sure. Fine. Everything's fine," said Donna, her voice plaintive.

"How are you and Randy doing?" Dad spoke so low Heather could scarcely hear him.

"We're doing great," said Donna quickly. "Why are you two asking all these questions?"

"We're just concerned about you—and Randy," replied Mom gently. "We're afraid you

45

may be—getting too serious about each other."

"What your mother is trying to say is that you two are spending too much time together. And we think you may be getting too—physically involved."

"Is that what this is all about?" demanded Donna. "Randy and I aren't going to do anything wrong. We're in love."

"In love?" echoed her father sharply.

"But you're both so very young—" her mother began.

"Weren't you ever in love, Mother?" challenged Donna. Her tone had a shrill, uncontrolled quality to it.

"Yes, I've been in love," was the firm reply, "and I still am."

"Well, then you must know how I feel," said Donna, still sounding strained.

"But, honey, I think there are more things we should be discussing about love and relationships with boys."

"Mother, I know more than you think. I don't see where there's anything for us to discuss."

"Before things get any more heated, I think we should sit down and pray together about this," said Dad. "You know, Donna, your mother and I want the Lord's best for you."

Donna's voice sounded vaguely morose as she said, "Please, not tonight, Daddy. I just can't pray right now."

Heather had heard enough. She stole quietly to her room. She felt ashamed for eavesdropping. But she was more disturbed than she cared to admit by the tension between her sister and her folks. She had never known a time when Donna wasn't willing to pray with the family.

Heather sat down on her bed and mused aloud, "Why can't Donna still be like Emily in the school play—all starry-eyed and blissfully in love? Why should being in love make a person moody and hard to get along with?"

During the next few days Heather's thoughts were distracted from Donna and Randy. She was busy with other things. She went skating with Pam, helped her mother clean the kitchen cupboards, and wrote a long overdue letter to her Grandmother Blake in the northern part of the state.

But on Friday evening something peculiar happened. Donna returned home early from a date with Randy. Her face was ashen, her eyes enormous with unshed tears. Without a word to anyone she went straight to her room and to bed.

Heather's parents were watching TV in the living room. They exchanged baffled glances as they heard the bedroom door shut.

"Shall I go talk to her, Jeff?" queried her mother.

"No, Meg, let her be," said Dad, sounding vaguely frustrated. "It may be nothing at all. This time, let's let her come to us."

A little later, when Heather went to bed, Donna appeared to be asleep. As Heather quietly slipped under the covers, she noted that Donna looked placid, composed. Heather felt mildly reassured. But sometime in the night she awoke and heard Donna sobbing inconsolably into her pillow.

47

7

The phone rang early the next morning. Heather ignored it. She was busy washing her hair. Finally she shouted, "Donna, can you get that?"

No answer. The ringing continued, a persistent, shrill noise.

"Donna! Mom's out and I have my head in the sink. Get the phone, will you!"

Still no response. The jangling seemed more insistent. Heather wrapped a towel around her head and ran to the phone. "Hello?" she said, breathless.

"Hello. Is Donna there?" It was Randy. He sounded funny.

"I *told* her to answer this," sputtered Heather, putting down the phone. "It's for you, Donna. Randy."

"Tell him I'm busy," came the stifled reply from under the covers.

"Doing *what*?" demanded Heather impatiently.

"I simply can't talk!"

Heather marched to her sister's bed and stared hard at Donna. "Will you please go talk to your boy friend so I can rinse the shampoo out of my hair? I feel like one gigantic drip."

"I don't want to talk to him," said Donna, turning away.

"Why not?"

"Please, Heather, do I have to have a reason? Just tell him I can't talk now."

Reluctantly Heather shuffled back to the phone. "Why should I have to do Donna's dirty work?" she muttered to herself. Picking up the receiver, she shifted into her "cheerful" voice, and said, "I'm sorry, Randy. Donna can't talk now."

"It's urgent, Heather," said Randy. He sounded desperate.

"I—I'll give her your message," said Heather lamely. She hung up the receiver and trudged back to Donna. She felt guilty inside for putting Randy off. Glaring accusingly at her sister, she said, "Donna, you shouldn't involve me in this— this scheme of yours to avoid Randy."

Donna remained silent. She sat on her bed, brushing her hair with slow, precise strokes.

"He said it was urgent," persisted Heather, her hands on her hips.

"That's what *he* says," said Donna in a small, melancholy voice.

"But what if it is?"

Donna turned and gazed stonily at Heather. There were dark circles under her eyes. She looked exhausted. Heather felt a twinge of pity for her sister.

"Did you and Randy—break up?" she asked softly.

Donna nodded. "I gave him back his ring last night."

"Maybe it's only temporary," offered Heather encouragingly.

"No. It's over. For good."

At dinner that evening Donna told her parents the same thing. "I don't intend to see Randy again," she said flatly. When Mom and Dad questioned her, Donna promptly excused herself from the table and went to her room.

If Heather assumed that Donna would remain uncommunicative in the days ahead, she was pleasantly mistaken. During the next two weeks, Donna snapped out of her depression and became surprisingly cheerful. Her old self. She threw herself into a flurry of activities—social gatherings at church (avoiding Randy, of course), visits with school friends, jaunts to the library, and even a shopping spree with Heather.

The two girls had a fantastic time. They bought new sports outfits, tennis shoes, cardigan sweaters for fall, and Donna's favorite—a bag of gourmet peanut-butter-flavored jelly beans.

"Those jelly beans cost more per pound than steak," teased Heather as they rode the bus home from town. The huge, creaking vehicle bounced and jarred and shook them until their teeth rattled.

"Tell me," countered Donna, "how often do I splurge on my peanut-butter jelly beans? How could I refuse them when they're so hard to find?"

"All I know," returned Heather practically, "is that the plain old licorice ones are cheaper."

"Ugh!" said Donna. "They turn your teeth black!"

"So? Yours give you peanut butter breath."

The two girls laughed suddenly as they realized how ridiculous their argument sounded.

"You're OK with or without black teeth," said Donna with a smile.

"And I really don't mind peanut butter breath," said Heather, flashing an affectionate grin. Growing momentarily serious, she added, "This is like old times, isn't it—the *best* of old times?"

Donna nodded. Her eyes were glistening. "You know what we should do?" she said suddenly. "Hike to the woods like we did when we were kids."

"Oh, yes," said Heather gleefully. "We can look for rabbits and squirrels—"

"And pheasants and blue jays and woodpeckers—"

"I can't wait!"

"Then how about tomorrow?"

The next day Heather and Donna packed a picnic lunch and hiked to the nearby woods. As they made their way through the thick brush and prickly twigs, Heather said, "Remember the time we got into poison ivy?"

"That was your fault," replied Donna, laughing accusingly. "You thought you were picking Mom a pretty bouquet."

"Well, you didn't have to help me carry it home."

"I was as dumb as you—and older too," admitted Donna with a chuckle.

The girls found their favorite place, a clearing near a huge gnarled oak tree. They spread out a blanket and eagerly helped themselves to the

51

sandwiches and fruit in the basket. As they ate, they sat back and gazed with pleasure around them. The sun was warm and gave everything a golden hue. The air smelled fresh and clean, like new grass, sweet cornfields, and dark, rich earth. The sky was a mass of billowing clouds, moving, changing, becoming castles, fantasy cities, and imaginary sculptures.

"Every cloud is a work of art," mused Donna, studying the constantly shifting formations.

Heather nodded, swallowing a mouthful of ham on rye. "God is a great artist, isn't He? He sure made a terrific world for us."

"Trouble is, we don't stop to see it," said Donna pensively. "We don't make the best of what God gives us. Sometimes we really blow it."

"I guess we do," said Heather vaguely. She wasn't sure what Donna was talking about.

"I've made up my mind," said Donna fervently, "to make something of myself. It's hard—when you've made mistakes—but I want to be the best person I can be for the Lord."

"That sounds good," murmured Heather.

Donna's dark eyes were nearly piercing now. "I'm going to try for perfect grades in my senior year, and maybe win a scholarship for college. I've been thinking a lot about college lately."

"I guess it's not too soon," said Heather. "It's just a year away. But I hate to think of you going away to school."

"I've been thinking about acting as a profession, too," continued Donna. "I know it won't be easy. But if I do really well in the senior play, maybe next year I'll be accepted in the summer

52

playhouse out at the lake." She breathed a sigh of anticipation. "I know I can be a good actress, Heather. Someday I want to be in Christian films. Maybe that's what God wants for me."

"I bet He does," agreed Heather, catching Donna's excitement. "You're a terrific actress. Just wait till the world sees what you can do."

"Like I said, it won't be easy," said Donna, randomly pulling a blade of grass. "The competition will be stiff, and it'll be a lot of hard work. But I won't give up. I won't let anything stop me."

Heather thought inadvertently of Randy and wanted to ask her sister just what place he had in her brave new plans. But Donna hadn't mentioned Randy's name in over two weeks. It was almost as if he had never existed. So Heather dismissed the idea of mentioning him now.

Donna was still talking about her renewed dedication to acting. "I won't think of anything else," she said resolutely. "I'll have just this one goal in life."

Heather could no longer stifle the question irritating her mind. "What about Randy?" she blurted.

Donna looked momentarily stricken. Then her eyes narrowed as she said with conviction, "I've forgotten him, Heather. I've put him out of my mind. Boys only complicate a girl's life."

Heather emitted a low whistle.

Leaning forward confidentially, Donna warned, "Don't you get interested in boys too soon, Heather. They just mix you up."

Heather felt a keen, puzzling disappointment. "But you said being in love was so great, like

53

magic—like Emily in *Our Town*."

Donna gazed soberly at the sky. She placed a blade of grass between her lips. For a long time she sat very still and very silent. Then in a sad, self-absorbed voice, she said, "When you're in love, Heather, you can't think straight. Sometimes it's scary—scarier than you ever dreamed."

8

One Sunday morning late in July, Heather was awakened by delicious breakfast aromas wafting into her room. She got up, pulled on her robe and slippers, and scuffed to the kitchen. Mom stood by the stove fixing pancakes and sausages.

"Sure smells good," said Heather, moistening her lips hungrily.

Meg flipped a pancake with a quick, smooth motion. "I figured it was time we had something besides oatmeal and toast." She glanced at Heather. "Would you please set the table, honey?"

Taking her time, Heather laid out plates and silverware on the orange flowered tablecloth. Then she took butter and syrup from the refrigerator. She smiled, recalling something special. "Mom, remember how you used to make us pancakes in the shapes of animals?"

"I sure do," chuckled Meg. "I had quite a time making little dogs and cats out of pancake batter, but that was the only way you and Donna would eat them."

Heather giggled. "I remember the time you played that real funny trick on Donna and me."

Mom looked up curiously. "What trick? When?"

"On April Fool's Day—years ago. Donna and I couldn't figure out why you made us pancakes on just an ordinary day. We found out soon enough."

"Oh, yes," said Meg, her eyes twinkling. "That was the day I poured the batter over little circles of cloth. That trick did go over rather well, if I do say so myself."

"Those were the toughest pancakes in the world. Donna and I tried and tried to cut them, but we couldn't."

"You two girls looked so frustrated, trying to cut through that material. I could hardly keep a straight face."

"Donna and I vowed to get even," laughed Heather, "but we never did."

Meg looked around with a questioning glance. "Speaking of Donna, isn't she up yet?"

"No," replied Heather. "When I got up, she was still sawing logs. She's getting lazier every day."

"No smart remarks, young lady," said Mom with a chiding little smile. "Just go get her up. I'd like to make it to church on time."

Heather helped herself to a bite of sausage, then returned to her room. Donna was still asleep.

"Hey, lazy bones, it's time to rise and shine," said Heather, shaking Donna's shoulder.

Donna rolled over with a disgruntled murmur and pulled the covers tighter. Heather shook her again. Donna mumbled something unintelligible under her breath.

"You'd better get up right now," insisted Heather, "or I'll dump a pitcher of ice water down your neck."

Donna sat up and shook her head groggily. "It can't be morning yet," she complained, her voice still fuzzy with sleep.

"It's morning all right—and almost time for church."

"I'll never make it," Donna muttered, climbing out of bed in slow motion.

"You look awful," observed Heather. "Feeling OK?"

Donna rubbed her stomach uncertainly. "I don't know. I feel blah."

"Maybe you're hungry," offered Heather brightly. "Mom is fixing pancakes and sausage. Don't you smell them?"

"Yes, I do," groaned Donna. Her face turned startlingly pale. "I'm not at all hungry."

"You must be kidding," exclaimed Heather. "Usually we get yucky old oatmeal, but today we're having pancakes smothered in butter and syrup—"

"Heather, please, I don't want to hear it!"

"—and those neat little link sausages. I tried one, and—"

"Oh, Heather, I'm going to be sick!" Donna clasped her hand over her mouth and dashed for the bathroom.

Heather stared after her in utter bewilderment.

Several minutes later, Donna returned. Her hair was straggly and damp around her face. Her eyes looked sunken, weary. "I must have the flu," she told Heather as she climbed back into bed. "Tell Mom I'm skipping breakfast and staying home from church today."

Heather's mouth contorted slightly. "If you

have the flu, I'll be next. You know how it always goes through the whole family."

"It wasn't my idea," muttered Donna. "Go ask Mom if she has any ginger ale."

Each morning for the next seven days Heather expected to wake up with the flu. But it never struck. Actually, Donna seemed to be hoarding it all to herself. Every morning she felt ill, but by afternoon she was up and around, herself again.

"That's the strangest flu I ever saw," Heather told Donna the following Sunday morning. "It comes and goes. Just when you think it's gone, it hits again."

"I know. It's totally unpredictable," grumbled Donna tiredly. "Mom thinks maybe it's a virus, or mono."

"Mono?"

"Mononucleosis."

"What's that?"

"Well, they call it the—the kissing disease, but that doesn't mean anything," scoffed Donna.

"Oh, oh," teased Heather. "You'd better check. Maybe Randy has it too." She remembered too late that Randy was an unmentionable word lately. To cover her blunder, she asked quickly, "Is Mom taking you to the doctor?"

Fortunately, Donna ignored her hapless remark and replied, "Mom wants to take me, but I don't want to go."

"Why not? Maybe then you'll get well."

Donna shook her head. "Mom would take me to Dr. Chapman, our pediatrician."

"So? He's nice. We've gone to him all our lives."

58

Donna looked perturbed. "I'm too old now, Heather," she said flatly. "I'm not going to sit in the waiting room in one of those little painted chairs with a bunch of screaming kids."

Heather's brow furrowed reflectively. "I never stopped to think that we could outgrow Dr. Chapman."

"Well, I have," said Donna. "So you tell Mom I'm going to rest today, and tomorrow I'll be as good as new."

In spite of Donna's optimism, on Monday morning she was sick again.

"You'd better tell Mom," warned Heather.

Donna shook her head vigorously. "No, and please, Heather, don't you say a word either. I don't want the folks to worry. I—I know I'll be feeling better any day now."

"You keep saying that."

"But it's true."

"Then how come you just threw up this morning?"

"I don't know. But right now I feel better. By tomorrow I'll be my old self again."

But she wasn't. A second week ended with Donna still suffering bouts of nausea. Mostly in the morning.

Heather felt increasingly frustrated and concerned. Donna had sworn her to secrecy about the prolonged illness. *Why doesn't Donna want Mom and Dad to know how she really feels?* Heather wondered. *What kind of weird game is Donna playing?*

Then, one ordinary, sun-washed afternoon, Heather found out. She sensed immediately that her world—and the world of her entire family—would never be the same.

Out of the blue, Donna burst into their room with an expression of stunned agony. Tears spilled out of her eyes as she stared desperately at Heather. "What am I going to do?" she sobbed. "I just found out. Oh, Heather, it's the worst thing possible. I—I'm going to have a baby!"

9

"I can't believe I told you just like that," said Donna when she had dried her eyes and regained her composure.

Heather stood speechless. Her hands at her sides felt like dead weights. Her sister's words couldn't be true. Surely at any moment Donna would laugh and nudge her and say, "It was just a joke, silly. Can't you take a joke?"

But the look on Donna's face told Heather this was no joke. This was real—terribly, painfully real. "How did it happen?" Heather wanted to shout. *Howhowhow!* Something in her head said, *It's a mistake. Not Donna, not my sister!*

"You must be wrong," she said imploringly.

Donna shook her head. She stared at the floor. "No. I went to a free clinic downtown. I had a test. It's definite."

Heather felt something turn over in her stomach. She felt numb inside. Numb and cold. She tried to find her voice. "What are you going to do?"

"I don't know." Donna sat on her bed gazing blankly at her hands. "I never thought it could happen—it couldn't happen to me."

"Who else knows?"

"Only you."

Heather caught her breath. She felt as if she had been running a long time. "You haven't told Randy?"

"No. I could never tell him."

Heather's thoughts raced. She sat down beside Donna and said quietly, "You'd better go tell Mom and Dad."

Donna looked entreatingly at her. "No, Heather, I can't. I couldn't bear to see their disappointment in me."

"They have to know. They just have to."

The emotion left Donna's voice as she said, "This woman at the clinic talked to me, a counselor. She said most girls these days get abortions. I know a girl at school who got pregnant and she had an abortion. Her parents never even knew. They thought she spent the weekend with a girl friend."

Heather's mouth dropped open. "An *abortion?*"

"Yeah. She acted like it was no big deal. She said she'd do it again if she had to. But her sister told me she cried every night for weeks afterward."

"Donna, you—you wouldn't—"

"Get an abortion? I don't know, Heather. The counselor talked about it so easily. Her voice was smooth as glass, and she just kept smiling, like she was talking about the weather or something. I sat there feeling this bitter cold inside me, right to my bones. I was petrified. I still am. Just the thought of an abortion scares me to death." Donna rubbed her hand unthinkingly over her

62

stomach. "I mean, wouldn't I be—killing the baby?"

"Oh, Donna, you can't do that. You've got to go tell Mom and Dad. They'll know what to do."

Donna sat motionless for several minutes, staring into space, absorbed in her own private thoughts. Just when Heather felt as if she could tolerate the silence no longer, Donna stood up and walked to the door. "I'll tell them," she said in a small, sad voice. "But in my own time—and my own way."

Two evenings later, after an hour of listening to records in her room, Heather decided to go to the kitchen for a snack. Glancing from one room to another, she wondered, *Where is everyone?* Then, as she passed the den, she caught a glimpse of Donna and her folks talking in low, serious tones. Suddenly Mom looked up and, seeing Heather, she came and shut the door without a word.

Heather felt a surprising hurt. *Why did Mom shut me out?* It was clear from her mother's expression that Donna had told them about the baby. *Did they think I don't know? Don't they want me to share this difficult time with them?*

Maybe they need to be alone with Donna for a while, Heather reasoned halfheartedly. She fixed herself a snack—a bologna and peanut-butter sandwich and potato chips—and settled down on the living room couch to watch TV.

A half hour later the den door opened and Donna and her parents came out. Heather looked up expectantly. She could see that Donna and her mother had been crying. Her father's face was stern. No one said a word.

Heather sank down into the couch and pretended to be engrossed in her program. The hero was about to get into a fight with a bad guy. No, two, three bad guys were surrounding him. He was licking them all.

Meg approached and stared reproachfully at Heather. "Young lady, you know you're not supposed to eat out here without a TV tray," she said severely. "A lot of good it does me to clean house with you kids always messing it up."

Heather looked up and snapped, "Don't worry. I'll pick up the crumbs!"

"Never mind, I'll do it myself," Mom continued, vigorously brushing off the sofa. "You girls just won't mind, will you!"

"Meg!" interrupted Dad sharply. His voice softened. "It's OK, sweetheart. Heather will go to the kitchen and eat."

Silently Heather picked up her half-eaten sandwich and chips and stomped out of the room. She didn't dare say anything. She might explode.

What happened? she wondered desperately. *Why is Mom worrying about a few crumbs at a time like this? Donna's the one she should be mad at, not me. Sometimes grown-ups don't make any sense at all!*

For the next two days the Blake household was uncomfortably silent. Mom went around with a pinched, worried expression; Dad developed a permanent scowl; and Donna avoided everybody.

It's the craziest thing, reflected Heather. *Everyone is trying to pretend that nothing's the matter.* Heather wanted to tell her folks she understood why they were upset, but she couldn't bring herself to say the words. So she pretended too.

The next afternoon, as Meg and Heather sat shelling peas on the back porch, Meg looked over and said vaguely, "One of these days we have to have a talk—"

"If it's about Donna, I already know," Heather replied woodenly.

Mom's eyes widened with surprise. "How—who told you?"

"Donna. Days ago."

"I—I wish you didn't have to know."

"Why not? I'm not a kid anymore."

Her mother reached over and squeezed her hand impulsively. "Oh, honey, you are to me. I wish I could spare both my girls all the hurts and pains—"

"You can't, Mama," said Heather faintly, her voice barely a whisper. She felt suddenly as if she might cry.

Her mother withdrew her hand and looked away. "I know. I know I can't always protect you." She looked back and forced a little smile. "I—I'm sorry about the other night. Blowing up at you over a few crumbs on the sofa. I was just so upset about Donna."

"That's OK," mumbled Heather. *It isn't really OK,* she thought. The hurt was still there. *But Mom has enough to worry about.*

"We'll be going away for a while this evening," her mother continued, trying to sound normal.

"Where?"

"Over to the Gordons'."

"Randy's parents?" exclaimed Heather. A whole row of peas overshot the bowl.

"Yes, we need to discuss things—make some decisions."

"What time are we going?"

Her mother looked over quickly. "Oh, not you, honey. Just your father and Donna and I will go. You understand, don't you?"

"Yeah, sure. I'd just be in the way."

"No, that's not it. It's just that there are things we need to talk about, privately. We won't be gone long. I could have Mrs. Morton from next door come over if you like."

Heather stuck out her lower lip. "No way. I'm too old for a baby-sitter."

After dinner that evening Heather watched Donna listlessly run a comb through her hair and dab makeup under her eyes to hide the shadows.

"Mom says I can't go with you," Heather mumbled sullenly.

Donna looked at her, her eyes narrowing. "I wish *I* didn't have to go."

"How come? Aren't Mom and Dad going to work things out?"

"I—I have to face the Gordons. Randy says they want me to have an abortion. They don't want their son's good name ruined. But I've thought about it over and over, and I know now I just can't hurt the baby. It's *somebody*, Heather. Someday it'll be a real person like you and me. How could I stop that? But the Gordons will hate me, I know they will."

"But Randy will be there. He loves you."

"Right now he's just plain scared. As scared as I am."

"Maybe he'll want to get married," said Heather hopefully. "Wouldn't everything be OK then?"

"No!" said Donna bluntly. "Even if he did want to marry me, I couldn't marry him."

"But why not? It could be the answer."

Donna pulled at a snarl in her hair. "I've tried to imagine us being married, Heather, and I know we're just not ready. There's school, for one thing. Randy would hate me if he couldn't go on with his education, and maybe I'd hate him for being tied down. And neither of us has any money. How could we live, let alone take care of a baby?"

"I guess it would be pretty hard," admitted Heather.

Donna yanked her comb harshly through the unrelenting tangle. Heather could see by her expression that it hurt. "Randy and I made a big mess of things," confessed Donna. "And just look how I've hurt Mom and Dad. That really kills me, too. I never dreamed that what we did could hurt so many people."

"I guess you hurt yourself most of all," said Heather sympathetically.

Donna smiled grimly. "Thanks for understanding, kiddo."

"That's OK," said Heather. She felt sorry for Donna, but she also felt an unexpected satisfaction that her older sister chose to take her into her confidence and share her feelings. It was more than Mom and Dad were willing to do. "Mom and

Dad haven't said a word to me about the baby or anything," she said aloud. "Every time I enter the room, they stop talking."

Donna scowled. "That's because the folks don't want to admit that such a thing could happen to a Christian girl in a nice Christian family."

Heather stared intently at her sister. "Donna," she began hesitantly, "I wonder, too. How could it—I mean, how could you *let* it happen?"

Donna walked to the closet and took out her brown velour sweater, a present last Christmas from Grandmother Blake. She flung it casually around her shoulders. Then she turned and looked squarely at Heather. For a minute neither girl said a word.

Then Donna's shoulders sagged slightly. Her lower lip began to tremble. "Oh, Heather," she said, her voice nearly a sob, "I didn't expect it to happen. I never wanted to do anything wrong. I mean, I know the—the facts of life, even about the Pill and all that." She glanced toward the bookcase. "You remember the little book Mom gave you to read on your twelfth birthday? Well, she gave me that book, too. And we had films in gym class. And all my life in Sunday school I've heard that Christians should be good and pure—"

"Then how—how could you?" asked Heather gravely.

Donna absentmindedly twisted a button on her sweater. Her voice grew very soft. "I've asked myself that again and again, and part of it is that no one warned me."

"What?" asked Heather, moving closer.

"No one told me how I would feel," said Donna slowly, "or how powerful my emotions would be when I was with someone I liked a lot. I always assumed I could control my feelings. I didn't expect them to be so strong."

Heather tried to think of something to say in response, but her mind was a blank. She wasn't sure what Donna was talking about.

Donna continued speaking, but now she wasn't looking at Heather. "Even though Randy and I are Christians, we convinced ourselves that we were a special case, that God wouldn't mind what we did if we loved each other. We wanted to believe it, so we did. We told ourselves that we had as much right to be together as—as George and Emily in Grover's Corners."

Donna reached for a tissue from the bureau and blew her nose. When she looked back at Heather, tears were making her makeup run. She said sorrowfully, "I knew afterward that it wasn't right, that we had broken God's law. I felt just awful. It was like someone had put a terrible weight on my heart."

Heather felt like crying with Donna. She wanted to comfort her, but she didn't know how. Donna might think she was a silly kid if she tried giving her a hug. The matter was settled anyway when Donna turned and glanced in the mirror.

"Oh, no, my mascara is running," she exclaimed, and dabbed quickly at her eyes with the tissue. Then she walked to the door. Without looking back, she said briskly, "I've got to go. Mom and Dad are waiting."

Heather remained in her room until she heard

the automobile pull out of the driveway. Then she walked slowly through the house, moving reflectively from room to room. The silence around her seemed very loud. She was alone, and lonely. She felt as empty inside as the empty house.

She walked over to the large picture window and stared out at the darkening sky. Urgently she whispered, "Dear Lord, please be with Mom and Dad and Donna. Help them to know what to do." She paused. "And Lord, help me not to feel so—so—whatever this feeling is I feel."

Usually praying made Heather feel better. But not tonight. Tonight she was painfully aware that her family was in the middle of a crisis—and at this moment she was being excluded from the family circle.

10

The last weeks of August passed much too quickly for Heather. Suddenly it was fall, September. School would begin in a few days. She would be an eighth-grader.

There was everything to do to get ready. New clothes to buy, old ones to repair, shoes to polish, and school supplies to purchase. Maybe Heather would even try a new hairdo—a short, curly style to replace her long, straggly mop.

Donna was getting ready too. But not for school. She was packing her clothes to go to Grandmother Blake's in the northern part of the state. Grandmother Blake lived all by herself now, a widow in a big, old house. The same house Dad had lived in as a boy. Heather couldn't remember much about Grandfather Blake, except that he had a booming voice and laughed like Santa Claus. She recalled spending one Christmas with her grandparents when she was very small. Grandfather Blake had dressed up in a red outfit and white beard and carried a pillow case full of toys. He said, "Ho-Ho-Ho," and swung her in his arms. Even now he was still Santa Claus in her memory.

Grandmother Blake was a quiet, gentle woman

who always seemed very wise. She never laughed like Grandpa, but her eyes twinkled when she smiled. Donna was lucky to have a neat place like Grandmother Blake's to stay. Well, it wasn't really luck, of course. Mom and Dad had done a lot of thinking and planning, and they decided Donna should stay with her grandmother until the baby was born.

Actually, it was just as much Donna's idea. Mom and Dad had told her she could stay home and have the baby. But Donna said, "No way." She didn't want to face her friends and classmates or the people at church. She wanted to go somewhere where nobody knew her. Well, almost nobody. Grandmother Blake's was the perfect place. Donna loved her old house with its nooks and crannies filled with all sorts of mysterious, old-fashioned things. Heather had always suspected that Donna was Grandmother Blake's favorite grandchild, being the firstborn and all. Grandma Blake didn't even raise her voice when she learned about the baby. According to Mom, she just said, "Meg, dear, if there's anything I can do to help, you let me know."

On the Saturday before Labor Day, Heather helped Donna pack her suitcases. That afternoon Dad would drive Donna to Grandmother Blake's and he would return home alone on Sunday.

Dad was anxious to get started so they wouldn't have to drive at night. He kept glancing in the doorway and looking at his watch. "Grandma will have dinner for us if we get there by six," he told Donna.

"Daddy, I can't close my suitcases," she whined.

"That's 'cause you're taking half the house with you," said Heather. "But I'll sit on them if that will help."

"You?—Heather *Feather?*" snapped Donna. "You're as light as a pin."

"I'm *not* Heather Feather! Just because that dumb Bobby Cooper calls me that."

"I'm sorry for being in such a crummy mood," Donna said contritely after Dad had shut the suitcases. "It's just that I feel so uptight." She gazed seriously at Heather and her father. "I want you both to know, I know that what Randy and I did was wrong, and I've asked God to forgive me. I believe He has, but that doesn't erase what happened. And it doesn't change what I'll have to go through." She clenched her hands as tears glinted in her eyes. "I admit I'm scared. Everything is going to be so different in my life."

Dad stepped forward and gave her a brief but tender embrace. "You know your mother and I are with you, honey," he said huskily. Before she could reply, he picked up the suitcases and went out. Heather figured he didn't want them to see him weep.

When he had gone, Donna looked glumly at Heather and said, "And it's going to be so different just living away from home, away from all of you."

"But you always liked Grandmother Blake's," Heather volunteered.

"Yes, I know. But I wonder if she'll still think I'm her special girl."

"Sure she will." Heather hoped she sounded more positive than she felt. Who really knew how Grandma Blake felt about her granddaughter having a baby without being married, and giving the baby to strangers? Maybe she felt just like the Gordons and wished Donna would have an abortion. But no. Grandma Blake would be on the baby's side.

Heather was both glad and relieved that Donna was going to go ahead and have the baby. But she wasn't sure how she felt about Donna's giving the baby away. It seemed a shame to give away a perfectly good little baby—a relative—Heather's own little niece or nephew.

Mom and Dad and Donna had talked about the possibility of keeping the baby. Dad said the choice was Donna's. But he reminded her of the big responsibility she would have for many, many years if she decided to raise the baby herself.

They also talked about what was best for the baby. Everyone agreed that the baby should have two parents who could give it a happy, stable home. There was no way Donna could do that.

A few weeks earlier, Dad had checked with a Christian adoption agency in Grandmother Blake's city. The people there said they would place Donna's baby with a nice Christian couple who couldn't have children of their own. They said Donna would be making some couple very happy.

So Donna agreed that the baby would be adopted. She admitted it was the only sensible thing to do. But Heather wondered how certain Donna really felt about her decision. No one had

74

actually asked for Heather's advice, but if they did, she would tell them she would never let anyone take away *her* baby.

"You're sure in another world," remarked Donna as she stacked the last of her books and record albums in a cardboard box.

"Oh, I was just thinking," said Heather, looking up with a start.

"Well, stop thinking and look and see if I've forgotten anything," said Donna, glancing around.

The room looked lopsided with Donna's stuff gone. Heather felt a twinge of loneliness already. "All I see is your big panda bear on the bed." She reached for the stuffed animal.

"No," said Donna determinedly, "leave it here. I'm too old for that sort of thing."

Heather nodded. She remembered too late that the bear was a present from Randy. But the panda wasn't the only reminder of Randy that afternoon. Just as Dad was packing the car trunk, Randy himself arrived. Heather couldn't believe he would dare to show up now. Donna seemed surprised too, and a bit dismayed, although she didn't say much. She didn't even make Heather leave the living room while they talked.

"I—I just wanted to give you these," he said, handing Donna a bouquet of red and pink roses. "They're from my mother's garden. I remember that you liked them, so I wanted you to have some—to take with you."

"Thank you," replied Donna in her formal voice.

Randy leaned nervously on one foot, then the other. He reminded Heather of a pawing stallion ready to bolt. "I guess that's all," he said stiffly. "I just thought I should come by." His voice lowered a notch. "I feel real bad, Donna. I—I wish there was something I could do." He paced back and forth aimlessly, as if arguing with himself. "If only I had some cash, maybe we could have worked something out. But, man, I can hardly keep my wheels going, let alone trying to support a wife and kid. You know how it is, Donna. It just costs too much to live these days."

She eyed him stonily. "I know, Randy. You don't have to explain."

He reached out to touch her arm, then let his hand fall limply. "I still love you," he said softly.

Donna looked away. "It's too late, Randy. We've both changed. Everything has changed." She took a deep breath. "You'd better go now. My dad's waiting for me. We have a long drive ahead of us."

Randy glanced around uncomfortably. When his gaze momentarily met Heather's, she quickly pretended to be busy stuffing some items into Donna's cosmetics case. *I didn't hear a word,* she wanted to say. *Forget that I'm even here.*

Randy seemed to do just that as he reached out and gently touched Donna's face. "I'm sorry if I upset you," he said. "It's just that I honestly don't know what to do or say." For one long moment he gazed woefully at her. "I sure am sorry," he said again in a small, strangled voice. He took several steps backward and bumped the arm of a chair. Then he turned quickly, sprang for the

76

door, and nearly ran across the yard to his car. Heather watched out the window as he drove away. He never looked back, not once.

Heather turned from the window just as Donna tossed her the bouquet of flowers. "You can have these," she said bitterly, fighting back tears. "I already have enough to remind me of Randy."

A few minutes later, Heather and her mother solemnly stood on the front porch and watched the family automobile pull out of the driveway and disappear down the street. Heather felt a lump in her throat. She had considered urging Donna to change her mind and stay home, but it was already hard enough for Donna to leave. So she had simply hugged her and said good-bye.

Heather and her mother stood watching long after the car was out of sight. "Maybe we should have gone with her," said Mom, her voice wistful.

Heather shrugged. "I don't think Donna would want the fuss of all of us going."

Meg squeezed Heather's shoulder and managed a smile. "I hope you're right, honey." As the two walked back into the house, Mom said brightly, "How about if we make a mushroom pizza for dinner? And since there's just the two of us, we'll eat in the living room and watch TV."

"Great," said Heather, following her mother to the kitchen. She knew they both sounded more enthusiastic than they felt.

For the next two days Heather felt an aching sense of desolation. She hadn't realized how deeply she would miss her sister. She found it hard to sleep. Her room seemed empty, unnaturally silent. She tried praying herself to sleep that first night. It helped, knowing Jesus was with her just as He was with Donna, miles away. But she felt relieved when her father returned on Sunday and said that Donna was comfortably settled at Grandmother Blake's.

Still, Heather needed someone to fill the void left by Donna. So on Labor Day she telephoned Pam and invited her over for dinner.

"I'm sorry, Heather, but I've already made plans to go on a picnic with Dave Powers." Pam's voice took on a lilting quality as she added, "Don't you dare tell anyone, but Dave is my steady guy now."

"Aw, there goes my best friend—down the tubes," Heather grumbled to herself as she hung up the phone.

Her mother looked up and said reassuringly, "You'll have a chance to make lots of new friends when you start back to school tomorrow."

Heather glanced over at her mother. She was sitting at the desk writing a letter to Donna. Tentatively Heather said, "I wonder if anybody knows about—about Donna."

Meg looked thoughtful, her pen poised over the paper. "I don't know," she said. "I hope there won't be talk."

"The church kids will wonder where Donna is."

"You'll just have to tell them she's staying with her grandmother for a while."

"They'll want to know why."

"I suppose you could say she wanted a change of scene after breaking up with Randy."

"But what if they guess? What if Randy says something? I can't lie—"

"No," said her mother quickly. "You can't lie.

78

But if people ask questions, you can try to change the subject. Or simply say nothing." She sighed heavily and added, "But I suppose eventually the truth will come out. We'll just have to trust the Lord for whatever happens."

Heather took the round pizza pan from the cupboard. "I'll just die if everyone finds out," she muttered.

But to Heather's immense relief, the first week of school passed without incident. And no one at church seemed suspicious over Donna's absence. "If anyone knows, they aren't letting me know they know," she told her mother on Sunday evening.

"Well, I hope you can settle down to studying and forget Donna's problems for a while," advised her mother.

"That's just what I'm going to do," Heather resolved.

But forgetting was easier said than done. The following Saturday morning, while Heather was pulling weeds in the front yard, Bobby Cooper sauntered over with his usual smug expression. The first thing he said was, "Where's Donna? I haven't seen her around lately."

"What's it to you?" retorted Heather, not looking up. She gave one stubborn weed an especially energetic tug. It shot out of the ground, its roots spraying dirt in the air. Heather nearly toppled over. Bobby leaped back in surprise.

"Boy, Heather Feather, you sure are a messy girl," he said with a malicious grin.

"What rock did you crawl out from under?" snorted Heather, brushing herself off.

Bobby laughed. "You can't make me mad, Heather Feather. I'm beyond such childish behavior."

She eyed him with disgust. "I suppose you're acting so high and mighty just because you're a ninth grader now."

"Well, it's certainly better than being a lowly eighth grader."

"Well, I like eighth grade just fine!"

"You would."

Heather's patience was exhausted. "Bobby Cooper, go home!"

He sat down beside her and reached casually for a blade of grass. "So where's Donna?" he said again, more quietly. "The kids at church are asking."

Heather's shoulders sagged. She stared at the ground. "Donna's staying with my grandmother up north," she said, as if reciting something memorized.

"How come?"

"She—she wanted a change of scene—you know—after Randy—"

"But this is her senior year—the *big* one."

Heather felt tears swimming in her eyes. "She wanted a change of scene—"

"You already said that."

Heather began to cry.

Bobby sat up on his knees and stared at her. "I'm sorry, Heather," he said, sounding genuinely apologetic. "Please don't cry. I can't stand to see a girl cry."

"I can't help it." She sniffed.

Awkwardly he patted her arm. "Don't feel bad,

please. I shouldn't have opened my big mouth. I understand, Heather, really."

She looked at him through wet lashes. "You couldn't possibly understand."

Bobby sat back and examined a scrubby weed. Slowly, elaborately, he pulled the weed apart, piece by piece. "I've heard rumors, Heather," he said.

"What rumors?" she asked, her voice breaking slightly.

"About Donna. Why she went away. About the baby."

The tears started again. "You know? How could you know? Oh, if you know, then the whole world must know!"

"I haven't said a word, cross my heart," said Bobby firmly. "Besides, what does it matter who knows?"

"Oh, it does matter. It changes everything. How can I face everybody?"

"What Donna did has nothing to do with you," argued Bobby. He tossed the fragmented weed aside and stood up. "Come on. Let's go."

She looked up, puzzled. "Go? Go where?"

"To the drugstore for ice cream. My treat."

Heather stood up and shook her head. "I can't—"

"You'd better. I may never offer to treat again."

"I—I shouldn't go anywhere with the likes o' you—" she objected.

"Oh, you like-a me? Well, I like-a you too," he wheedled, coaxing a smile.

She laughed in spite of herself. "OK," she said finally. "Just let me go tell Mom and grab a tissue."

When Heather returned from the drugstore an hour later, she rushed excitedly into the house and exclaimed, "Mom, guess what! Remember how I always thought Bobby Cooper was such a creep? Well, you know what? He's practically a human being!"

Her mother looked up from the dress she was mending and smiled. "I always suspected that, honey."

"I mean it, Mom," said Heather breathlessly. "He actually treated me like a person. We talked and he bought me ice cream, and for the first time ever he didn't act like a brat."

Mom smiled tolerantly while Heather paused to catch her breath. Suddenly Heather felt self-conscious. She certainly didn't want Mom getting the crazy idea that she liked Bobby or anything dumb like that.

"I better go do my homework," she said abruptly, and headed for her room. She smiled privately. *Imagine, volunteering to do my homework on a weekend, without Mom having to yell at me or anything. Maybe I'm going crazy and just don't know it yet.*

But in spite of her attempt to be studious, Heather couldn't keep her mind on pronouns, participles, and gerunds. She found herself remembering how surprisingly easy it had been to share her bottled-up thoughts and feelings with Bobby. Of all people to listen so patiently—and he actually seemed to understand! Was it possible that Heather had found a new friend in the most unlikely of places—in the funny, unpredictable person of Bobby Cooper?

11

During the first week of November, Heather wrote her sister a brief, newsy letter, saying:

Dear Donna:

I'm sorry I haven't written sooner, but I've been very busy. I like eighth grade, except the work is harder. You won't believe this, but I have a "new" friend—Bobby Cooper. I *said* you wouldn't believe it! Remember how I couldn't stand him? Well, I guess getting older must agree with him, because he's much nicer now than he used to be. We go skating and to the drugstore for ice cream, and we sit together in church sometimes. But we make it look accidental, so the other kids won't make smart remarks about us liking each other.

Mom says it's all right for Bobby to be my friend, but I can't go out alone with a boy, like in a car, until I'm fifteen. That's OK with me. Besides, Bobby can't get his driver's license for at least two more years. I'm not saying I like Bobby for a boy friend or anything like that, but it has been awfully lonely around here since you left. Also, my best friend Pam has a steady boy friend now, so I don't see her much. So Bobby is someone to talk to.

Guess what, Donna. I'm finally really growing up! In two weeks I'll be thirteen. A teenager. Almost a woman. Finally, last week I traded my undershirts for a pre-teen bra. Mom wasn't convinced it was necessary, but she said OK, if that's what I wanted. Now if only my body will get the idea. I'm tired of being a string bean. I'm just afraid that maybe I'll never grow. Does that happen sometimes? The other thing I wanted to tell you is that I've got my period, what Mom calls her "monthly friend." It happened last week too. That's what gave me the courage to pack away my undershirts. I told Pam, but she acted like it was no big deal. She said she went through all that stuff over a year ago. Well, it's a big deal to me, but I wouldn't admit it to anyone but you.

I'm glad you like living at Grandmother Blake's (at least as much as possible, considering). I knew you'd still be a "special person" to her. I hope you're feeling OK. We all miss you like crazy.

Love, Heather

Within a week Heather received a reply from Donna:

Dear Heather:

I was so glad to hear from you. I miss you and Mom and Dad and our house and my school and everything! How I wish I could be at home like usual, seeing my friends and looking forward to the school play. As I wrote to Mom, Grandma Blake is super. But it's still not the same as home. I'm taking some correspondence courses so I won't have so much to make up, and I'm working a few hours a day at a bakery near here. The lady who owns it is a friend of Grandma Blake's. It's sort of fun, but I have to be careful not to eat the profits.

I'm happy to hear that you're practically a woman now. Just don't grow up too fast. I'm just beginning to see that there are lots of years to be grown-up, but not so many to be a kid.

I have some exciting news, too. Yesterday I felt the baby move. It was just a little flutter in my tummy, but for the first time my baby is real to me—something (someone!) that actually exists. I can't describe how it made me feel. I tell you, I hate to think of the day I have to give my baby up. I'm not sure I can.

I'm glad you and Bobby are friends. Still, keep an eye on him. After all, he is a boy.

Have you seen Randy? No, don't answer that. I don't want to know.

Well, I'd better close now and get to work. I love you—and Mom and Dad too. Pray for me. I pray every day for you.

Love, Donna

When Bobby came by that afternoon to walk Heather to the roller rink, she told him about her letter from Donna. "She says she doesn't want to hear anything about Randy, and I'm glad. I won't have to tell her we saw him with another girl." As Bobby took her hand companionably, she added with conviction, "Donna's going to be OK. She's busy studying. And she even has a part-time job in a bakery."

"Now that's the kind of job I could go for," said Bobby, smacking his lips.

"Me too. I bet I'd gain a hundred pounds."

He glanced approvingly at her. "You're fine just like you are."

"Oh, yeah? Well, I'm no Pam."

"Aw, she's too fat for me."

Heather gave him a suspicious look. "No boy thinks that. You're just saying it to make me feel better."

"So? It worked, didn't it?"

They had nearly reached the rink when Bobby took her other hand, turning her to face him. "When you get your school picture, I want one," he said. "Autographed."

"We'll see how they turn out first," replied Heather. "I know they'll be positively awful. The photographer pushed us through like an assembly line. *Snap*—next!—*snap*—next!"

"I know," agreed Bobby. "I had my tongue in my cheek when he snapped me. My face probably looked like crazy putty."

Heather looked puzzled. "Why would you pose like that?"

"Pose, nothing! I was trying to find a place to put my gum."

"Well, I hope your picture turns out, because I want one."

"For a dart board?"

"What do *you* think?"

They exchanged impish grins, then continued walking, swinging their clasped hands between them.

Just before Thanksgiving, Heather wrote Donna another letter. She said:

Donna, I think Bobby and I are becoming a little more than friends. Sometimes he holds my hand when we go for walks. We skate arm-in-arm at the roller rink. He passes me little notes between classes. And we talk on the phone every night.

Lately Mom has been giving me some disapproving glances. She thinks I'm too young to like a boy. What do you think, Donna? I'm thirteen now. I do like Bobby alot. But I'm confused too. How can I like Bobby when just last year I couldn't stand him? Has Bobby changed, or have I?

One more question, Donna. Don't think I'm stupid, but I don't know who to ask besides you. What should I do if Bobby tries to kiss me? I don't even know how. Pam used to practice kissing the back of her hand, but that seems dumb to me. Is there a book that tells how? I'm not saying I plan to kiss Bobby, but I'd like to be prepared for— someday.

Surprisingly enough, "someday" arrived even before Heather's letter reached Donna. On the Sunday evening after Thanksgiving, Heather rode home from church with Bobby and his parents.

They stopped at Harvey's Ice Cream Shoppe for sodas. Mr. Cooper treated.

When the Coopers dropped Heather off at her house, Bobby got out too and told his dad, "You can go on home. I'll walk. I'll be there in a minute, OK?"

Then, as he walked Heather to her door, he slipped his arm around her. The night was beautiful. He mentioned that fact and she readily agreed. A beautiful night. The first snow of the season had fallen that afternoon, covering the ground like powdered sugar. The air was cold and crisp.

Heather noticed right away that Mom had forgotten to turn on the outside light, so the porch was dark. Obviously Bobby noticed, too. Just as she reached the door, he bent over and awkwardly brushed her lips with a kiss. Before Heather realized what had happened, Bobby was striding back down the sidewalk, whistling happily.

Heather entered her house in a daze. Imagine, her first kiss! She felt enchanted. It didn't seem possible that just last summer she had vowed never to kiss a boy. When her mother asked if she had had a good time, she dreamily murmured, "Yes—wonderful," then drifted off to her room.

The next morning at the breakfast table, Meg handed Heather a bowl of oatmeal and remarked, "So you enjoyed going with Bobby and his parents last night?"

Between mouthfuls, Heather said, "Uh-huh. Mr. Cooper is funny just like Bobby. He tells lots of jokes."

Mom sat down across from Heather. She looked concerned. "You like Bobby a lot, don't you?"

Heather squirmed in her chair. She scooped in larger spoonfuls of oatmeal.

"Am I right, Heather?"

"Maybe."

Meg cleared her throat and said brightly, "Would you like to help me make our homemade Christmas tags today, Heather, after school?"

"What fun will that be with Donna gone this year?" she said darkly.

Her mother stood up and began clearing the table. "I know we both miss Donna very much," she said reflectively, "but the two of us could have a nice talk while we work, if you're willing."

Heather nodded without enthusiasm. "Maybe tonight after dinner, OK?"

After the dinner dishes were done, Meg placed last year's Christmas cards, pinking shears, hole punchers, and spools of ribbon on the table. "Do you want to cut or punch?" she asked Heather.

"Cut."

Without apparent interest Heather took the pinking shears and began cutting a card, trimming away the unnecessary parts. She trimmed the inside of the card to match, snipping away the name of the sender. "This will do," she said, handing it to her mother.

Meg took the two parts of the tag, punched holes in the top and tied the tag together with green ribbon. "All done," she said, sounding pleased. Heather handed her another tag.

Meg paused and gazed at Heather. "I'd like to

89

talk about you and Bobby," she said seriously. "I have the feeling you two are becoming—more than friends."

"So that's why we're making Christmas tags tonight," snapped Heather.

"Don't you think you're seeing too much of him, honey?" Meg continued. "Why, when I was your age I wasn't allowed to date at all."

"I'm not you," mumbled Heather. "All the girls in eighth grade date now."

"I just don't want you becoming involved with a boy when you're still so young."

Heather glared at her mother. "Why don't you say it? You're afraid the same thing will happen to me that happened to Donna."

"That's not so," said Meg defensively. "I just want you to know what you're doing."

Heather began to cry. "What you mean is, you don't trust me. You think I'll do something wrong!" She jumped up from the table, upsetting the box of cards, and ran to her room. She flopped down on her bed and sobbed. The worst thing about her outburst was that she wasn't even sure why she was bawling. Her feelings were all jumbled, confused.

A moment later Meg entered the room and sat down quietly beside her. "Can we start over?" she asked gently.

Heather sat up and reached for a tissue on the night stand.

Her mother smoothed the bedspread absently as she said, "I realize now that I made a mistake with Donna."

"You mean by letting her date Randy?"

"No. By not sitting down and talking openly with her about boy-girl relationships and the problems she would face. I don't want to make that same mistake with you."

Heather looked up uncomfortably. "I—I already know all that stuff, Mom."

"Do you, Heather? Our society certainly bombards us with sex in every movie, magazine, and billboard, but their message is very misleading."

"What do you mean?"

"They try to tell us we don't need moral standards, that we can do as we please without feeling guilty or suffering the consequences. That's not so." She looked carefully at Heather. "I think most young people would rather have some limits and guidelines set for them, so they wouldn't have to worry so much about what they should or shouldn't do. Especially as Christians, we need to see sex from God's point of view."

Heather's expression fell. "Oh, Mom, is this going to be a sermon?"

Meg smiled tolerantly. "Don't you want to know what God thinks of sex?"

Heather frowned. "I guess He doesn't approve—"

Meg laughed heartily. "Oh, honey, that's not true. Why, the very first sexual thought was in the mind of God Himself. It was His idea!"

Heather's eyes widened. "It was?"

"And since God created sex, it's very precious to Him," said Meg. "He wanted a special love for two people to share who are set apart for each other for life. He even made marriage to be a life-size illustration of Christ's love for the church."

Meg was silent for a moment, then she continued. "When sexual love is part of God's special plan, it's beautiful and good. The problem comes when people misuse it, when they don't save that special love just for marriage. Then they hurt themselves, and other people, and God."

"Like Donna?" Heather looked soberly at her mother. "But Donna didn't plan to do anything wrong. It just happened. How do I know it won't—just happen—to me, too?"

"There aren't any easy answers, honey, especially these days when many people behave as if there's no difference between right and wrong. They live together without being married. They say it's all right to have sexual relations with someone you're only dating. But God says no, that's wrong. He wants you to stay pure not only for your future mate, but also for Him. You see, your purity is very important to God."

"My purity? Why?"

"Let's put it this way," said Meg, shifting her position to face Heather. "You know how quiet and respectful we are when we enter the church sanctuary."

"Yes, because it's God's house."

"Well, that's true in a way. But God's house, His temple, is really within our own bodies. When we accept Jesus as our Savior, His Holy Spirit comes and lives inside us."

Heather nodded. "My Sunday school teacher says that's why we should respect our bodies and not do anything to harm them."

"That's right," said Mom.

Heather wrinkled her forehead thoughtfully.

"But Donna said she couldn't help what she did. Her feelings were too strong. What if someday I feel the same way?"

Mom nodded. "Someday you will face the same feelings, honey. But I hope you are more prepared for those feelings than Donna was."

"How can I be prepared?"

"First of all, I hope you will make the positive choice to remain pure for your future husband. It doesn't matter how strict your dad and I are or how many rules we impose, ultimately, you alone must decide what you will do."

Heather looked apprehensively at her mother. "Wow! It sounds sort of scary and confusing. How can I be sure I'll do what's right?"

Meg thought a minute. Then she said, "Look at it this way, honey. Dating and marriage are like a stairway with a very special secret room at the top. That room is a treasure a man and woman bring to marriage to share only with each other. The stairs leading to that room are the steps a person climbs toward marriage."

Heather looked baffled. "What are the steps?" she asked.

"Well," said Meg, "the first step might be just a glance or a smile. The next step could be conversation; sharing your thoughts and feelings. Then a touch; holding hands; a kiss; an embrace. The higher steps, prolonged kissing and petting, are for the purpose of arousing each other or getting ready for lovemaking. The thing to remember, Heather, is that it's easy to climb the steps, but very difficult to go back down."

"I'm not sure I understand," said Heather.

"Here's an example," Meg explained. "If a girl gets used to kissing a boy, then holding hands will no longer seem so exciting. Each step prepares you for the next step up."

"Does that mean you shouldn't kiss a boy?"

"Not at all, honey. Kissing is very natural and enjoyable."

"Could I get pregnant like Donna—just by kissing or being close to a boy?"

"No. You can only get pregnant by having sexual relations. But if you kiss and pet each other, you may become so excited that you go all the way up the stairs without intending to."

Heather nodded. "Donna said that's what happened to her."

"The point is," concluded Meg, "each step is special and should be taken slowly. Some girls and boys want to rush right up the stairs, but then they miss so many good things along the way."

Heather was perplexed. "How do you know which step you're supposed to be on?"

Meg smiled. "A good question, honey. When you are dating casually, your physical contact should be somewhat limited. The more serious you become, the more you will want to express your feelings physically. But if your physical sharing runs ahead of your emotional, spiritual, and intellectual sharing, the growth of your relationship becomes lopsided. You hurt each other and grieve the Lord."

"That sounds like a bummer," said Heather. "I remember hearing an older girl at school complain that her boy friend never talked to her or took her anywhere. All he wanted to do was make out. Is that what you're talking about?"

"That's the general idea," said Mom. "Still, Heather, only you can decide what limits to set for each stage in a relationship. Just remember that each step up the stairway brings sexual intimacy that much closer. You can minimize temptations by staying on the lower steps. And keep God's plan in mind; that special room at the top is reserved for marriage. That's your treasure to give your husband someday."

Heather solemnly rolled her eyes toward the ceiling, imagining a special room at the top of the stairs with a gold-lettered "reserved" sign on the door. She felt a prickly sensation under her skin as she wondered what person God had that room reserved for. Whoever he was, Heather wanted to guard *his* property—with God's help, of course!

"Thanks, Mom," she said, slipping into her mother's arms for a quick hug. She wanted to add, "Thanks for treating me like someone more than a little kid," but she had a feeling her mother already knew. So instead, she simply said, "If you want, we can go back now and finish the Christmas tags."

12

The busy days of December tumbled by pell-mell, one after the other, leaving Heather nearly breathless. She wondered if she would ever finish her Christmas shopping, or complete her science project, or get her book report done in time. And what about the letters she owed Donna and Grandmother Blake? Worst of all, there was hardly time to think of what Christmas was all about.

Before going to bed on Christmas Eve, Heather looked out her window at the white, sparkling landscape. The dark star-flecked sky made the snow look almost blue. It was a perfect night.

"Happy Birthday, Jesus," she said aloud. "I've been doing some thinking lately, and I've decided You and I need to have more talks. Sometimes I almost forget You're real. I forget You're right inside me ready to help me with my problems. I'm sorry I've ignored You lately. I really want us to be best friends. Help me to be the person You want me to be. I love You." She turned from the window, then paused and glanced back. "Oh, Lord Jesus, I almost forgot. Merry Christmas!"

Early Christmas morning Heather and her parents drove upstate to Grandmother Blake's for a four-day visit. Heather was overjoyed to see Donna again, but she couldn't help noticing her sister's swelling tummy. Still, Donna looked rosy-faced and healthy. The two girls sat talking for hours every day, catching up on the past few months. But their time together was all too brief.

In fact, it seemed to Heather that the entire Christmas holiday passed with alarming speed. Suddenly it was January—the dreariest month of the year. Heather's spirits sagged. Only her occasional outings with Bobby and the young people's gatherings at church broke the tedium of blizzards and books.

Then came February—a brighter month if only because her friend Pam was throwing a big Valentine's Day party to celebrate her fourteenth birthday. The upcoming party was the talk of the entire eighth grade class.

Ever since Christmas Eve, Heather had been having regular conversations with God. Just before bedtime she would sit down in the chair by the window, look out at the sky and talk out loud to the Lord. She told Him whatever was on her heart: how her day had gone, what someone had said or done, her problems and worries of the moment. For Heather, the one advantage of Donna's absence was having the room to herself, a private place to pray.

In the past, Heather's faith had meant little more to her than church attendance and being with other Christians. To her, God had been primarily a "community project," a rallying point for the church. Of course, Jesus was her Savior, but she had worshiped Him from afar. He hadn't seemed someone personal like Mom and Dad or Donna. But now that she was spending time alone with the Lord, talking and sharing and even studying His Word, she was discovering the special friend He really was.

So as the day of Pam's Valentine's party approached, it was natural for Heather to talk to God about it. "Dear Jesus, I'm so excited," she said. "This will be my first real boy-girl party. Bobby is taking me. Oh, Lord, please let everything be perfect!"

Pam's party started out just as "perfect" as Heather had anticipated—for the first two minutes. As Bobby and she entered the Morrows' gaily decorated basement recreation room, Pam stepped forward and welcomed them, laughing giddily. "Heather, you look beautiful!" she gushed; then looking at Bobby she added loftily, "And you don't look bad—considering."

"And you look the same as always, Pam," he grunted. "Ugly," he added under his breath.

"The room looks absolutely gorgeous," Heather cut in, hoping that Pam hadn't heard Bobby's snide remark.

"Oh, well, Dad helped me decorate the place," said Pam, her attention diverted. "And wait'll you see my cake. It's huge, with red candy hearts all over. I think it's so neat to be celebrating two occasions at once, don't you?"

"I'd like to see that cake," said Bobby hungrily.

"Don't you ever think of anything besides food?" snapped Pam.

"Not if I can help it."

98

"Well, maybe someday you'll turn into a giant jelly doughnut."

"That's better than being a butterball," Bobby shot back.

"Please, don't let me keep you from the refreshment table," said Pam coolly. She turned away in a huff.

Bobby steered Heather toward the punch bowl. "I still don't like that girl," he muttered, glaring back at Pam.

"Then you're even," said Heather dryly. "Remember, this is her party. Try to be nice."

After several glasses of punch and half a dozen chopped ham sandwiches, Bobby moved away from the refreshment table. Heather sighed with relief as they finally mingled with the other couples. Some of the guys and girls were playing Valentine party games. Several boys were gathered around the stereo, arguing over which record to play next. A few couples were dancing self-consciously. Several girls who had come without dates stood in a corner talking impassively. Once in a while they looked enviously at the gyrating twosomes.

Pam interrupted the proceedings long enough to open her presents. Her mother had insisted that she specify only inexpensive "fun" gifts on her invitations. Heather had been at Pam's house when Pam had stormed and complained—to no avail. Now, reflected Heather, Pam had to sit there and pretend to be excited over a bunch of dumb gifts. The boys all gave Pam an assortment of joke and gag gifts: clacking false teeth, squirting rings, leaky water glasses, rubber snakes, and dime store novelties. The boys delightedly experimented with their prank offerings, while the girls stifled their giggles and tried to look the other way.

As the evening progressed, the music grew louder, the lights lower, and the couples bolder. Many danced languidly now to romantic ballads. Others had drifted off to corners of the room to neck. Heather glanced around nervously. Pam wafted by in Dave Powers's arms.

"Where are your folks?" Heather whispered.

"Upstairs," said Pam. "I made them promise not to come down unless there's a riot."

Heather looked for Bobby. He was staring sullenly into the punch bowl.

"What's the matter? Spot a goldfish?"

"No. Taste this."

Heather sipped the drink and choked. "It tastes awful!"

"Yeah. Someone must have just spiked the punch. And the sandwiches and cake are gone. Now what's there to do at this dopey party? Everyone's dancing or off somewhere smooching."

"What should we do?" asked Heather timidly.

"Well, I'll try dancing if you want, but I warn you, my dad says I got feet the size of gunboats." He winked teasingly. "Besides, if I have my choice, I'd rather smooch."

Heather felt her face growing warm. "I—I don't know—"

Pam swayed by again and called, "Come on, Heather. Try some of these new steps. Have some fun!"

Heather looked disconcertedly from Pam to Bobby. "What time is your father picking us up?" she asked.

"Eleven. Why?"

She gazed around the room once more, then replied, "I'd like to go home now, Bobby. Would you mind calling your dad?"

"I'm sick of this place myself," said Bobby. He reached for her hand. "We have plenty of time. We could walk home, if you'd rather."

Later that night Heather sat by her window and prayed quietly. "Jesus, I'm puzzled. Tonight I had a good time and a bad time. I'm not sure how I feel about all the things the kids were doing. I just know when I looked around, I felt sad and lonely. I wanted to come home and talk to You. I guess tonight was one of those times of choices Mom talked about. Lord Jesus, I hope I did OK."

As February dissolved into March, Heather thought more and more about her sister. In just a month or so Donna would be coming home and life would be wonderfully back to normal. Heather could scarcely wait. She missed Donna more every day.

Now that Heather was really growing up, she and Donna had so many more things to share than when Heather was just a kid. Would Donna notice the changes? Heather hoped she would. Every night before she went to sleep, she prayed, "Dear God, bring Donna home soon."

One afternoon during the first week of April, a week before Donna's baby was due, Heather returned home from school to find her mother packing.

"Where are you going, Mom?" she asked, setting down her books.

"I'm going tomorrow morning to be with Donna when the baby's born. You knew I was planning to go."

"But so soon? You still have a week."

"Grandmother Blake called. The doctor said the baby might come early. I want to be there."

"I wish Dad and I could go, too."

"So do I. But you have school and your dad has to work. You two will have to take care of each other while I'm gone."

"When will you come home?"

"It may be a week or two—or more. Whenever Donna's ready." Mom forced a smile. "Do you think you can manage without me?"

"I guess so," said Heather, "as long as Dad doesn't mind living on TV dinners and take-out food."

"Well, it won't be forever," said Mom, "and I'll call you just as soon as the baby comes."

Three days later, Heather received a long-distance phone call from her mother. "Honey, is Daddy there?" asked Meg.

"He's not home from work yet, Mom," replied Heather. "Is Donna OK?"

"Yes, she's fine. She had her baby this morning; a healthy seven-pound boy."

"Oh, a boy!" exclaimed Heather. "I wish I could see him."

"He's darling," said Mom wistfully. "He has Donna's dark hair and perfect complexion. Of course, he's a little red and wrinkled right now."

"Will you be bringing Donna home now?"

"Soon, honey. In a week or ten days. I want her to gain back her strength first. This is a difficult time for her, you know."

"I know. I'll tell Daddy you called. We miss you both so much."

After hanging up the receiver, Heather walked to her room and sat down by her window. She gazed out at the trees just beginning to blossom. The earth was shaking off winter like an old brown coat. It was coming alive again with color. *Spring is a time for starting over—for beginning brand new. That's what Donna will have to do.*

"Lord Jesus," said Heather softly, "lately I'm always feeling sad and happy at once. Is that my age? I used to feel just one way or the other. That was easier. Like right now I feel so sad that I'll never see my new little nephew. I wish I could hold him just one time. But I'm happy now, too. I'm so happy that Donna's coming home soon. Everything will be just like it used to be. Well, almost. At least, we'll be a family again!"

13

The next week passed with agonizing slowness. Finally, on Wednesday evening, Mom telephoned and said, "We'll be home on Friday. But don't mention it around. Donna doesn't want to see anyone just yet."

After the call, Heather told her father excitedly, "We've got to have everything just right for them on Friday—the house clean, a nice dinner ready."

He nodded. "I'll tell you what. I'll vacuum the carpet right now."

"Great! And I'll polish the furniture like Mom does when company's coming. We'll have this place spotless."

They worked for hours, father and daughter, cleaning, polishing, and straightening. "I didn't realize we had let so many dishes pile up," said Heather when she had put away the last skillet.

"And I'm glad your mother didn't see this stove the way it was," said Dad. "It's amazing how fast things get dirty."

At bedtime Dad kissed Heather good night and said pleasantly, "I think I've seen a minor miracle in this house tonight, honey. The place looks fantastic. I didn't know you were such a hard little worker. I'm proud of you."

Heather beamed. "Know what, Dad? Tomorrow night I'm going to bake a welcome home cake for Donna. Chocolate with fudge frosting. All by myself, OK?"

"Sounds great to me. I'm a chocolate fudge cake man myself."

Heather gave him an impulsive hug. "Oh, Daddy, I'm so happy. The day after tomorrow we're all going to be together again."

Dad simply nodded, holding Heather's head against his chest. When he released her, she saw there were tears in his eyes.

"I love you, Daddy," she said, as if somehow to comfort him.

"I love you too, sweetheart," he said, his eyes crinkling with a smile. "I thank God every day for our family."

When Friday afternoon arrived, Heather was bursting with excitement. She scurried around the house, making sure everything was in order, especially in her—and Donna's—room.

Dad got off work early and helped Heather fix dinner: meat loaf, scalloped potatoes, and a fresh green salad. The table was set and everything ready when the automobile finally pulled into the driveway.

"They're here!" Heather ran to the door and flung it open, crying, "Welcome home!" But when her eyes rested on Donna, she felt a momentary wave of shock. Donna looked— different, like an older, heavier version of herself.

"Come in, come in," Heather heard herself

saying. Automatically she embraced Donna, then Mom.

Dad hugged them both, too. He held Donna for a long time. She began to cry and buried her face against his shoulder. He kept patting her back and saying, "It's OK, sweetheart. It's OK."

At last Donna pulled away, wiped her eyes and tried to smile. "It's wonderful to be home," she said.

"I'm surprised," said Mom, looking around. "I think the house looks even cleaner than I left it."

"Thank Heather for that," said Dad.

"And Dad too," Heather added. "We both worked hard. You should have seen it *before* we cleaned."

"And I must say, something in the kitchen smells delicious." Mom's eyes twinkled. "I thought I might still have to cook when I got home."

"No," said Heather quickly. "Dinner's all ready. Dad helped me."

Meg headed for the kitchen. "You two have been regular little eager beavers."

"I'll help you serve," said Dad, slipping his arm around Meg's waist as they left the room.

Donna sat down on the couch and put her head back wearily. Heather sat down beside her. "I guess you're tired from the long trip, huh?"

Donna nodded.

"How is Grandmother Blake?"

"Fine. She sends her love."

"Oh, good," mumbled Heather. "Are you feeling OK now?"

"Pretty good."

"Good." Heather sighed and stared at her hands. There were so many things she had planned to say to Donna. Where were the words now? She wanted to ask about the baby, but she didn't know if she should. But how else could she find out what she wanted to know?

"Did you—did you get everything settled—with the baby, I mean?"

Donna closed her eyes. "Yes," she said tonelessly. "He's been placed in a Christian home."

"Did you meet the people?"

"No. The agency has a policy against that."

"But you—you saw the baby, didn't you?"

Donna opened her eyes, but she still didn't look at Heather. "I saw him a couple of times, just for a few minutes."

"Did you hold him?"

Donna's dark, sullen eyes met Heather's. "Yes, I held him once. They didn't want me to, but I insisted. I wanted to remember for the rest of my life how he felt in my arms."

Heather looked away quickly. She had trespassed, catching an unwitting glimpse of Donna's immense grief. She wanted to jump up and run.

"I named him, too," continued Donna quietly.

"What?"

"I named my baby. Jeffrey."

Heather's eyes widened. "That's Dad's name."

"Yes. The agency lady said the adopting couple would give him their own name. But he'll always be Jeffrey to me."

"Will you go back to school?" blurted Heather. She couldn't bear any more talk of the baby.

"School?" echoed Donna vaguely. "No, I won't go back, not with my class, anyway." Her voice took on a sad, reminiscing quality. "It doesn't seem possible that they'll be graduating in just six weeks. There'll be the class parties and the school play and the honor assembly." She looked somberly at Heather. "I would have graduated with honors, maybe even summa cum laude."

Heather realized in dismay that this subject was no better than the other one. "What are you going to do now, if you don't go back to school?" she asked haltingly.

Donna thought a minute, then said, "I'll probably go to summer school. With my correspondence classes, I'll have enough credits to graduate. I have to get my diploma. The folks still want me to go on to college."

"I think you should, too," said Heather with a nod. At least their conversation was on safer ground now.

"Mom and Dad are probably right, but right now I don't care about anything. I just feel tired."

"You'll feel better when you get back into the swing of things," said Heather, trying to sound optimistic.

"I'm not getting back into anything for a while," said Donna. "I told Mom not to expect me back at church for a few weeks yet. I don't want to face anyone, at least not until I get my shape back." She looked down in exasperation at her waistline. "I put on almost twenty pounds during the last three months, Heather. I was a real blimp."

"Well, you'll be your old self again in no time."

"No," said Donna, standing up, "I'll never be

my old self. I just have to figure out who I am now."

Before Heather could reply, Mom came out and called them to the table. Heather was just as glad she didn't have to respond to Donna's strange remark.

The family took their places around the table and held hands while Dad prayed. His voice caught as he said, "Thank you, God, for bringing our girl back to us." Then he said amen without even mentioning the dinner.

"You forgot to bless the food, Dad," said Heather.

"God will bless it anyway," said Mom.

"I'm not so sure. Dad and I cooked it."

"It tastes just fine," said Donna.

Heather glanced at her sister's plate. "Then how come you're not eating it?"

"I told you. I've got to get my figure back."

Everyone ate in uneasy silence for a few minutes; then Meg said, "You two really outdid yourselves with this meal. I may just retire and let you take over in the kitchen."

"Don't you dare," cried Heather. "I'm not ready for the domestic life yet." As she spoke, she caught a glimpse of Donna's expression. Donna looked miserable. "Did I say something wrong?" asked Heather meekly.

"No, of course not," said Dad. He reached over and squeezed Donna's arm. "Did you see Heather's surprise for you? Heather, why don't you get you know what."

Heather got up and took her chocolate cake from the cupboard and set it on the table. "I made it myself. It's your favorite, Donna."

"Oh, it's beautiful!" Donna looked as if she might begin to cry again.

"You don't have to eat any," Heather told her quickly. "I mean, if it'll spoil your diet."

"Of course she'll have a piece," said Mom cheerily.

"Yes, I want to," said Donna. "A small piece."

"Heather worked on that cake all last evening," remarked Dad.

For the next few minutes they all ate cake and smiled and talked nonchalantly. Dad made little jokes and they laughed at just the right moments. But they were trying too hard. Heather could see that. Things weren't the same as before. Nothing was the same. How could it be, when Donna had changed so drastically?

While they ate, Heather quietly studied her sister. Donna didn't look "sweet sixteen" anymore; now she was seventeen and ancient. She looked haggard and seemed to act and react out of an overwhelming exhaustion. She was more like Mom now, with that unmistakable settled, grown-up look. Even worse, her personality had changed. Her lively spirit was gone; she was subdued and withdrawn. *She's like a zombie,* realized Heather, horrified.

Immediately after dinner Donna went to their room. Heather followed timidly from a distance. There had to be something she could do to help or comfort Donna, to break through her shell of grief.

She cautiously eased open the bedroom door and peered around. Donna was lying on her bed, weeping silently into her pillow. Heather tiptoed in and sat down on her own bed across from Donna. She couldn't think of anything to say, so she just sat in silence, waiting.

"Do you want to be alone?" she asked when Donna's tears subsided.

"No, you can stay." Donna sat up and blew her nose.

"Are you OK?"

"Yeah. I—I was just—" She hesitated, twisting her tissue around one finger until the paper shredded. "I was just thinking about my baby."

"Oh." Heather's voice was barely audible.

"You should have seen him, Heather. He was so little. When I put my finger in his hand, he held on so tight. He held on like he would never let me go."

Donna looked up entreatingly. "How can I ever forget him, Heather? How can I start over? Where do I begin?"

"I don't know," Heather said shakily. "I don't know."

Donna lay back down and turned her face to the wall. Heather felt a sense of desperation tighten in her chest. *There's nothing I can say to help Donna,* she thought wildly. *I can't stay here watching her suffer. I can't!* She turned and fled out of the room.

Heather hurried to the den, shut the door, and telephoned Bobby. "I want to come over and see you," she said. She was trembling.

"What?" said Bobby. "Come over? You mean *here? Tonight?"*

"Yes," said Heather urgently. "Please. I need to

talk to you. Can I come?"

"Well, no, Heather, not tonight. My folks are out for the evening. They never let me have anyone over when they're gone."

"I don't care," said Heather resolutely. "I'm coming anyway." She hung up the phone before Bobby could reply and left the house without a word to her parents.

14

Heather ran all the way to Bobby's house. She arrived breathless, tears streaming down her cheeks, and pounded insistently on the door.

Bobby opened it a crack and stared at her in consternation. "Heather, I told you not to come," he hissed.

"Bobby Cooper, you let me in this instant!"

Grudgingly he stepped aside. "If my folks find out about this, I'll tell them you forced your way in," he muttered. Then he saw that she was crying and exclaimed, "What's the matter, Heather?"

"Oh, Bobby, it's so awful," she wailed, going inside.

"What happened?" he stammered, putting his arm around her shoulder.

"It's Donna. She came home today."

"Well, is she sick? Did something happen to her baby?"

Heather looked up at him. "She had the baby and gave it away, and now she's so sad. And she's changed so much. I don't even know her anymore."

Bobby steered her toward the couch and they sat down. "Donna's bound to be different, Heather," he said reasonably. "Look at all she's been through."

"But I thought once she got home everything would be all right."

"It will be, in time."

"No. Things are worse now than ever. The Donna I remember is gone. She's like a stranger now, and I can't stand to see her feeling so hurt. I hate it. I hate everything that has happened. If I could, I'd run away and never come back."

Bobby slipped his arm around her and drew her close. "Come here, Heather Feather." They sat like that for several minutes, her head resting against his shoulder. They hardly breathed. A radio droned on in the kitchen, playing popular music.

Gradually Heather's anguish dissolved. She felt good being close to Bobby. She felt warm and protected and cared for. The tension inside her was easing. "Thank you, Bobby," she whispered.

"What for?" he mused.

"For listening."

"That's OK."

"I don't know what I'd have done without you to talk to."

"I'm glad you came over," he murmured. He tilted her chin toward him. "I really like you, Heather."

"I like you, too."

Without warning he kissed her, slowly, tenderly. It wasn't a brief or casual kiss like before. It was warm and sweet. Heather found herself liking it very much. She wanted to kiss Bobby back. But should she? She began to pull away, but Bobby held her fast. She felt momentarily without energy, helpless. . . .

Then a thought occurred to her: *I'm not ready to be on this step yet. This step?* Where had she heard that phrase before?

Suddenly she remembered the illustration her mother had shared with her months ago. She had said that only Heather herself could decide when to climb which steps to that special "reserved" room at the top. This was one of the first choices of adulthood.

Heather pushed at Bobby and struggled to catch her breath.

"What's the matter?" he sputtered.

She shook her head. "We can't—"

"Please, Heather—" He drew her back and kissed her again. Another thought formed in Heather's mind: *I am Heather, my own person, the Lord's person. My body is His temple!*

She broke away from Bobby's embrace and scooted to the opposite end of the couch. They stared wordlessly at each other. Heather was trembling. She tried to find her voice. "Bobby, I—I like you a lot, and I want us to be friends for a very long time."

"Me too," he said with feeling.

Her voice grew stronger. "Bobby, I don't want us ever to do anything to spoil our special friendship."

He looked at her with a glimmer of comprehension. "You mean like Donna and Randy?"

She nodded.

"I wasn't thinking of anything like that, Heather," he said emphatically. "I just wanted to kiss you."

"But one step leads to another, maybe faster

than we think. I want to take the stairs slowly. I want to be able to appreciate each step."

"Stairs? Steps?" He frowned at her. "What are you talking about?"

She smiled. "Someday I'll tell you all about it. It's a long story, too long for tonight."

"So then, what about *us?*"

Heather absently twisted a strand of her hair. "Mom says real love means honoring God and each other." She looked earnestly at Bobby. "That's what I want us to do—what's best for each other. But I can't do it alone. I need your help, too."

Bobby stood up and walked over to a large oak desk. He picked up a book and turned it over in his hands. "I guess you're right, Heather." He looked sheepishly at her, embarrassed. "I'm sorry for coming on so strong."

"That's OK. I guess the only problem is—I liked it."

Bobby opened the book and thumbed rapidly through several pages. "You better go now, Heather," he said abruptly. "I've got homework to do."

She looked questioningly at him.

"Go," he said again, "before I change my mind."

"Good night, Bobby," she said, going over and lightly kissing his cheek. She walked to the door and glanced back. "Thanks again."

"Will you be OK going home?"

"Sure. I'll run all the way."

He followed her outside and said, "I'll walk you halfway, then watch until you reach your door."

When they parted minutes later, Bobby said, "Don't forget, Heather Feather, we're going skating tomorrow night."

"I won't forget," she promised. "I can't wait!"

Heather's parents were waiting for her when she entered the house. They were concerned about her absence. Dad had just telephoned Pam and was about to call Bobby's house when she walked in. In spite of their worry and displeasure over her misdeed, they listened patiently as she told them why she had gone out. "I feel lots better since I talked to Bobby," she concluded. She didn't mention the part about him kissing her, but maybe someday she would tell Mom. After all, it was what Mom had said that helped her make the right choice.

"We understand why you went out, Heather," said Dad, "but it was still wrong of you to leave without telling us. I'm afraid there'll be no roller skating for you tomorrow night."

"But Dad, I promised Bobby—"

"Then you'll just have to tell him you're sorry."

Heather nodded mutely, then said good night to her folks. She felt disappointed, but somehow the punishment seemed minor compared with all the other things she had experienced tonight.

She entered her darkened room as quietly as possible. Donna was sleeping soundly. Heather walked to the window and looked out. How she yearned to talk out loud to the Lord right now. She had so much to tell Him. Maybe she could just say the words in her mind. She sat down and gazed out at the sky. Wispy clouds were drifting in slow motion past the moon.

Heather felt surprisingly good inside. She was glad about what she had said to Bobby. God had given her the words to speak tonight. And He would always be there for her, ready to give her the courage to do what was right. All she had to do was ask.

Lord, I'm glad I have You to help me, she prayed silently. *I've learned from Donna's experience, and I know the choices won't be easy. At least I'm not facing those choices as blind and as unprepared as Donna was.*

She winced, thinking of her sister. *Lord Jesus, if only Donna could be happy again. Please help her. Please show me how I can help her too.*

It seemed an impossible request—finding a way to help Donna out of her misery. But God was God. Heather knew He would come up with something.

Early the next morning, a sunny Saturday in mid-April, Heather awoke with an idea. She and Donna would go on a picnic, like they did when they were kids. If anything could cheer Donna, that would. Heather lifted her eyes to the ceiling and whispered, "Thank you, God."

She dressed hurriedly and rushed to the kitchen to pack a picnic lunch. No one else was up yet. It was only 6:00 A.M. Quietly she hard-boiled half a dozen eggs, made sandwiches, sliced carrot and celery sticks, and filled a thermos jug with lemonade. She topped off the lunch with some olives, pickles, and potato chips.

At nine, Heather shook Donna and said, "Wake up, sleepy head. We've got big plans for today."

Donna rolled over and grumbled, "Go away. Let me sleep."

"No," said Heather, "We're going on a picnic. I have our lunch all packed."

Donna opened one eye. "A picnic? You're kidding!" She turned over and pulled the covers over her head.

Heather tugged at the covers. "Come on, Donna. This will be our first picnic of the year. We'll go to our favorite spot; the clearing in the woods by the big oak. Remember when we went there last summer? We had so much fun."

Donna sat up and looked grimly at Heather. "I told you I don't want to go anywhere and I don't want to see anyone."

"You won't see anyone in the woods. There'll just be the two of us."

"No—I don't think so."

"Please, Donna. I already packed the lunch."

Donna nodded reluctantly and climbed out of bed. "I might as well say yes. You'll wear me down anyway."

An hour later the girls, in corduroy jackets and jeans, were hiking through the nearby woods, swinging the picnic basket between them.

"Slow down!" cried Donna breathlessly. "I'm not ready to run the mile yet, you know."

"We're almost there," said Heather eagerly. "Look, there's the oak. Isn't it a beauty?"

"This place never changes," mused Donna. "It looks just like it did the last time we were here."

Heather breathed deeply. "That's what I love about the woods. You feel like no time has passed at all."

"Well, all I can think about right now is sitting down," said Donna.

Heather quickly spread a blanket out on the grass and they sat down with obvious relief.

"No place in the world smells as fresh and clean as these woods," said Heather, stretching out her legs.

Donna nodded. "I've always loved it here; the songs of the birds and the wind rustling the trees. Listen."

"It sounds like whispers."

"And look at the colors," said Donna softly. "It's spring—exploding like fireworks."

"You sound like a poet," noted Heather in surprise.

Donna smiled. "I tried writing some poetry while I was at Grandmother Blake's."

"Really? Can I read it?"

"No, I threw it away. It wasn't very good."

"Maybe it was," argued Heather. "You should have kept it."

"No. It was depressing. About Randy—and the baby."

"Maybe you'll write some more—some happy poems."

Donna squinted toward the sun. "No, I don't think so." She glanced sideways at Heather. "You don't understand how it is. You see, I don't feel like writing. I don't feel like doing anything at all."

Heather adjusted her position, tucking her legs under her. She watched Donna silently for a minute. Then casually she said, "Do you remember *Our Town?*"

"My class play? Of course. It was one of the

most important events in my life."

"Well, I finally finished reading the book."

"Oh?" said Donna without interest.

"I kept thinking about you, Donna," continued Heather. "You were always Emily in my mind."

"So?"

Heather ran her hand along the edge of the picnic basket. Back and forth over the rough rim. She was trying to think of just the right words to say to Donna, something to make a difference. At last she said, "Do you remember how Emily went back to Grover's Corners after she died?"

"Certainly I remember. I played the part, didn't I?"

"And how she felt such pain because people didn't appreciate what they had on this earth?"

"Yes, I know. That was my best scene," replied Donna wistfully.

Heather gazed earnestly at her sister. "Donna, Emily was dead and couldn't go back to her family. It was too late for her to appreciate life and love and rain and sunshine and all those good things." Heather sucked in a breath, gathering courage. "But it's not too late for you, Donna. You can come back. I want you back. We all do."

Donna sat quietly running her hand over the blanket, smoothing it, then making little folds, then smoothing it again. When she looked up at Heather, her eyes glistened with unspilled tears. "How can I come back?" she asked dismally. "I feel as dead as Emily, and just as far away from everything that matters."

Heather shrugged slightly. The words stuck in her throat. She coughed, willing them to reach her tongue. "I don't know the answer, Donna," she said haltingly. "But I'll—I'll be here for you. And so will Mom and Dad. And the Lord Jesus will help you—if you'll let Him. I know, because He's helped me with lots of things lately."

"Really? Like what?"

"Well, He's taught me a lot about choices."

"Choices?"

"Yes," said Heather. "He's taught me that I'm not helpless, that I can choose to do what is right—and He'll help me. You can choose too, Donna."

"Choose what? What's left for me to choose?"

Heather's voice rose with urgency. "You can choose not to be dead like Emily—to come back—to be happy again."

For a long minute there was only the sound of birds and the flutter of leaves. Then Donna leaned forward and lifted the lid of the picnic basket. "What'd you bring?" she asked, removing a foil-wrapped package.

"Those are carrot sticks," said Heather. "And there are egg salad sandwiches, and lemonade, and chips—"

Donna's forehead wrinkled in exasperation. "You definitely are not helping my diet."

"OK," said Heather, opening the package of carrots and celery, "you can have the *sticks* and I'll have the *chips*."

They both laughed, lightly, impulsively. Donna squeezed Heather's hand in a brief, affectionate gesture. "Thanks," she said softly.

"What for?"

"For—for whatever." Donna smiled gratefully.

"For a kid, you sure are getting smart."

Heather bit into an egg salad sandwich. Mixed with sunshine and fresh air, it tasted delicious. As she ate, she thought about the next time she would see Bobby. She had a lot to tell him. Mainly, that she had a feeling everything really was going to be all right now—for the two of them, for her family, and yes, even for Donna!

Moody Press, a ministry of the Moody Bible Institute, is designed for education, evangelization, and edification. If we may assist you in knowing more about Christ and the Christian life, please write us without obligation: Moody Press, c/o MLM, Chicago, Illinois 60610.